WHEN THE BRAVE ONES CRIED

Lee Dalton

Copyright © 1986
Horizon Publishers & Distributors, Inc.

All rights reserved. Reproduction in whole or any parts thereof in any form or by any media without written permission is prohibited.

Library of Congress No.: 86-081778
ISBN: 0-88290-282-2
Horizon Publishers Catalog & Order No.: 1967
First Printing, 1986

Printed and distributed
in the United States of America by

Horizon
Publishers
& Distributors, Incorporated
50 South 500 West   P.O. Box 490
Bountiful, Utah 84010-0490

This book is for
all the men and women with whom I've fought fire

Hiram Volunteer Fire Department - Ohio
Chief Wally Ellenberger and Stanley Ellenberger
who taught me how

Fredonia Fire Department - Arizona
Michael Holmes, my assistant chief

Kanab Volunteer Fire Department - Utah

Woodruff Volunteer Fire Department - Utah

Captain Jim Sanford, Phoenix Fire Department

and the many fire crews of
The National Park Service
and the United States Forest Service
who fought beside me when forests were burning

Chapter One

Y'know, if anyone had told me a year ago that I'd be a no-smoking, no-drinking, no-coffee, no-bad habits Mormon I'd have told them to go get their head examined. Man! It's been quite a year.

Chapter Two

Those first twelve weeks had almost killed me. I'd never done anything so difficult in my life. They call the place "The Grinder," and spending a summer there will grind you right down to nothing. Twelve weeks of climbing ladders, dragging hoses, and crawling into a flaming concrete tower in the scorching heat of summer while wearing nearly sixty pounds of protective clothing and breathing equipment had sure redistributed my weight. I was certain that there wasn't an ounce of fat left anywhere on my body.

Then, suddenly, all that was left were a few more minutes of sitting, stiff and starched, in my new dress uniform—a few minutes of sitting and listening while the mayor, a couple of councilmen, a few Department dignitaries and, of course, the Chief told all the world what a great bunch of heroes we were.

I didn't feel like much of a hero that warm September Friday afternoon. I felt more like a survivor. Of the thirty who had started the twelve weeks in The Grinder, I was one of twenty-three who made it. The Grinder had ground us up and spit us out—changed in many ways from what we'd been when we started.

The Chief finished his remarks. They began calling off our names, one by one. I stepped forward when mine was called and my mother pinned my new badge to the front of my jacket while my father stood back a step or so, grinning a broad grin. Linda pecked me modestly on the cheek and we all sat down again.

I couldn't help but sneak a few glances downward at the heavy silver badge. I have to admit that I felt a surge of pride. But I remembered, too, what the Chief had just said: "The last weeks have been hard, but the real test still lies ahead."

Tomorrow I'd head for a firehouse in the South Valley and the beginning of twelve months as a "Boot," a brand new probationary firefighter. I'd have no name other than "Boot" or "Booter." I'd get stuck with all the dirty work. I'd be watched carefully in all I did and said by the company captain and the others with whom I shared the house. I'd fight fire. I'd answer medical and rescue calls. I'd see death and suffering in almost all its forms. And I'd face death myself. I'd be proving myself—in every instance.

I have to admit it. I was nervous.

. . . .

The ceremonies were finally over. We changed into our street clothes and headed for one last "cold one" at Dudley's Shamrock Tavern, our favorite watering hole near the Academy. Linda sat beside me with the other wives and girlfriends that were at a couple of tables pulled together. We were washing the taste of The Grinder down with a free flow of beer when in the front door walked most of the training staff.

They came to our table, dragged chairs up alongside us and sat down. We chipped in to buy a round for them and began to discover that they were real people, too.

My head was buzzing from the beer when Chief Clark, the Battalion Chief in charge of training, leaned over and focused on my face with his rather bloodshot eyes. "What assignment did you draw?" he wanted to know.

"Engine Five, sir," I replied.

"Engine Five, huh? Good station. It's one of the busiest in the city. What shift?"

"A-shift, sir," I answered.

He belched. "A-shift at Five, huh? Damn good assignment. A busy station's a good place to learn. Dave Meaker's captain on A-shift. Damn fine man, Meaker, even if he is a nigger."

I sat, reflecting on that for a moment. I knew I'd have to work with Blacks when I got out, but the idea of having one for my captain bothered me. Ever since high school. . . .

My thoughts were interrupted by Stan Kojwalski. Kojwalski is a ladder company captain who also helps with training. He's a big man with a ruddy red nose and hair to match. He was also quite drunk. "Engine Five? Better watch it, boy. That's th' Mormon Battalion down there. Nearly everyone in Battalion Three is a Mormon. Better take your own coffee with you, 'cause you won't find much of it in Station Five."

"Be careful, Boot," said Bill Burke, another captain from the north end of the city. "Don't let 'em get you. Those damn Mormons are out to convert everybody. There's a lot of people go down there and come out the other end a Mormon." He laughed and poked the guy sitting next to him as he added, "And what would a fine little Irish Catholic girl like this do with a Mormon Polack like you?"

I laughed. "Don't worry. They'll never get me. After all, I used to be an altar boy."

They all laughed heartily at that until Ed Manor, one of my classmates who'd been nursing a glass of straight 7-Up, said quietly, "Oh, I don't know. Being a Mormon's not *all-that-bad*. I was a deacon once."

All eyes snapped up to look and him and Chief Clark changed the subject.

. . . .

Linda insisted that she drive me home. I sort of stumbled into the house and had to listen to another of Mom's talks about my drinking. I showered and crawled into bed, but I didn't sleep very well despite all the depressant in my blood stream. When I woke in the morning my head felt like someone was driving a ladder truck around and around inside it.

It was an awful day to start my new career.

Chapter Three

I drove toward the South Valley section of the city with my stomach churning and my hands sweating. I kept telling myself it was silly to be that nervous, but it didn't do any good. As I passed through the downtown section, my mind raced along thinking of all the things that were sure to go wrong. I tried to tell myself that I had been well trained. I knew what to do and how to do it, but a part of me just wouldn't listen.

The city is marked by contrasts. Just south of the downtown highrises is a section of tree-shaded streets with large, well kept houses, and spacious green lawns. The University comes next, then a large park, and finally, the freeway. Once you pass under the freeway you're in a different world. Green lawns and well-kept houses give way to weed-choked lots topped with dirty and squalid clapboard houses—houses filled with people who seem to have no place in the world I've always lived in. Almost as much as I was bothered by the idea of having to prove myself in my job, I was bothered by the idea of having to deal with the rainbow of people who lived down in the Valley.

Signs written in Spanish proclaimed stores and churches and welfare missions. Signs adorned shops advertising soul food and hair straightener. Other signs in Chinese, Korean, Vietnamese, and Japanese offered who-knows-what? Clusters of young men standing on street corners in the early morning regarded me cooly, almost hostily, as I waited uncomfortably at traffic lights. A few winos rested in stupor against the sides of buildings, and one derelict lay half-in and half-out of a gutter along the roadside.

Mexican low riders—those cars with suspension systems lowered until they drag the ground—rumbled in and out of intersections. Powerful engines of beat-up rods, driven by young Black men, competed for space on the roads. Blank windows of empty buildings and guard grates on occupied buildings, closed tightly against early morning, gave me the shivers.

I was entering a new world, and it frightened me somehow.

. . . .

I turned the corner onto West 26th at Dyer and wondered what ladies of the night in their thin, tight clothing were doing out at that hour of the morning. Then I saw the Cadillac parked nearby and noticed that they were turning over a night's take to their pimp. As I continued down Dyer, I finally turned in at West 30th and pulled quickly into the back lot behind a low brick building where a sign on the front proclaimed it to be Fire Station Number 5.

I dragged my coat, bunker pants, boots and helmet from the trunk and walked in the back door looking as confident as I could, which I don't think was very much. There were voices coming from the kitchen, so I headed there and found the men from C-shift gathered around the table. These men were with the men I'd work with on A-shift. The clock on the wall read 7:55.

"Well, here he is," one of them said, nodding toward me.

"Late, too," another chided. Handing me a folded flag, he said, "Booters put the flag up every morning and take it down every night. Department manual says it goes up at oh-seven-thirty. You're twenty-five minutes late!" I looked up at his olive-colored face and heard his Latin accent. My neck hairs rose, but I kept my mouth shut.

I could feel my face reddening as I took the flag and headed out the door. When I got back inside, the four men from C-shift were gathering their things to leave. The three I'd spend the next twenty-four hours with were seated around the table. One of them, a tall, powerfully built Black man with a little mustache, stood up and extended his hand.

"Come sit down," he said in a quiet voice. "I'm Dave Meaker, captain of this mess. This is Don Spencer, he's our engineer. This guy over here is Luis DeMonte who, as of today, is the senior firefighter."

They all shook hands with me. They seemed friendly enough, but I could feel their eyes searching me—sizing me up. As I shook hands with Luis, I knew that my palms were wet and clammy.

Captain Meaker took me to the storeroom and checked out a set of breathing apparatus. We walked back to the bay where our Engine stood waiting. "Take good care of it," he admonished as I set it carefully inside the left rear compartment of the Engine. "Your life depends on it."

The station had been built for two companies but was occupied by only one. Half the bay lay empty. I set my boots, with bunker pants carefully folded down around them, on the floor beside my place in the bucket on the right side of the Engine and hung my coat on the grab bar beside my rear-facing seat. My helmet was set on the engine cover between my seat and the seat where Luis would ride. I was ready, now.

We returned to the kitchen and sat around the table while the captain outlined the day's work for us. I looked around the room and sure enough, there was no sign of a coffee pot! I decided it would be better to do without than call attention to myself.

With the assignments completed, Captain Meaker said in a voice so quiet and gentle-sounding that it seemed out of place from a man his size, "Boot, we always start off the day by kneeling together for a word of prayer. You're welcome to join us if you want."

I couldn't think of a good way to say no, so I joined them as they knelt in a circle on the dayroom rug. I felt so ridiculously uncomfortable I was sure it must show on my face. I'd never heard of such a thing happening at any of the places I'd worked before—nor even imagined it!

Captain Meaker asked, "Whose turn is it?"

"Mine," Don Spencer said. They bowed their heads and I reached clear back to my days at St. Stephanie's and made the Sign of the Cross across my chest while Don began. "Our dear Father in Heaven," he said simply. "We give thanks for this day and the opportunity to serve our fellow men as firefighters. We're thankful for our families and ask thee to keep them safe while we are gone. And, Father, we ask thee to keep us safe during this shift." Then he added something that shocked me—something I never thought I'd hear from an action-loving firefighter: "And, Father," he added, "if it should be thy will, we pray that thou wilt watch over all those who live in our area that we might not have to run to help any of them today."

I stood up, feeling mighty silly about it all and followed the others to the store room.

. . . .

We cleaned the bunk room, bathroom, and locker room then climbed aboard the Engine for a day of inspection tours to some of the small manufacturing plants in the area southeast of the station. We toured buildings, mapping them as we went. We made note of special hazards, open shafts, chemicals, and the like until lunchtime when we stopped at a Wendy's to eat.

The afternoon was spent pulling hose down from the drying tower and rolling it up for storage. Then a rigorous game of basketball and an hour and a half spent working out and jogging around the engine bay brought us to suppertime.

All that, and not one single call. I was beginning to wonder if I'd heard right, that Engine Five was one of the busiest in the city.

We worked together on supper. I pulled the flag down right on time, then peeled the potatoes. The knife slipped while I was slicing them, and I knicked myself a little. I cut loose with a word or two reserved for that kind of occasion and then realized they were the first words like that I'd heard all day. I looked around and saw the others staring at me with looks that would wither flowers. I knew I'd have to watch my mouth around there.

When the table was finally set, we pulled our chairs up and sat down. That brought another shock. The bowls of potatoes, gravy, roast beef and vegetables were piled high and waiting on the table. As soon as everyone was seated, I reached out and picked up the nearest bowl and a spoon. Then I noticed everyone looking at me. Captain Meaker put his hand on top of mine and stopped me. "Would it be okay if we ask a blessing first?" he said quietly.

I dropped the spoon into the bowl and sat there wishing I could crawl in after it while Don Spencer said some words I didn't really hear.

Supper, like supper in most firehouses, was delicious. I sat listening to the others as they talked of their families and work they were doing in some place called "The Ward." I kept quiet, feeling like a complete outsider and hoping an alarm would hit soon so I could start taking my place in the social order of the station. These men were friendly enough, but there was still a barrier that separated us. I wanted to break through it—fast.

While we ate, I was secretly studying the others. Captain Dave Meaker was the man in charge on our shift. The captain was a tall man with heavily muscled shoulders and arms, a quiet voice, and skin so brown it was almost black. A few wisps of gray curled in with the black hair on his head. I guessed that he was in his early forties. He wore a ready smile and an air of confidence that made me decide he'd probably be a pretty good man to be with in a hot spot—even if he was, as Chief Carter had said, a nigger.

Don Spencer was a shorter, heavy-set man with no fat on him. His brown hair was beginning to grow thin on top, and his face was almost always serious. As our engineer, he drove the Engine and ran the pump. His voice reminded me of some of my father's recordings of a famous opera singer, and I bet myself that Don was probably a pretty good singer himself.

Luis DeMonte sat beside me, and I had a hard time sizing him up without being too obvious about it. He was smaller than the rest of us but powerfully built anyway. No weakling could possibly stand the department's required physical training program. Luis was only a year or so older than I was, but he had been out of the Academy for two years, and had been, until I arrived, the junior firefighter. He seemed to be enjoying his new status ahead of me, and I found myself resenting his attitude more than just a little. Ever since high school I've had a lot of trouble feeling comfortable around Mexicans, and when Luis had told me that morning, with his slight Spanish accent, to put the flag up, I'd started disliking him automatically.

My thoughts evaporated when I heard the captain asking a question about my family. I was just starting to tell him that I still lived with my parents on the north side when a loud tone, coming through the loudspeaker in the ceiling above our heads, cut me short. All talk stopped. Both the captain and Don pulled cards and pencils from their pockets and waited, ready to listen and write.

The voice from the speaker was steady and calm—almost mechanical—as it repeated the message twice. "Engine Five, Engine Three, Ladder Three, Battalion Three. Channel one assignment. 2600 South Copia—2600 South Copia. The La Casa Restaurant—fire in a fryer vent." As I set down my glass, I was appalled to notice that my hand was shaking.

No one ran. We walked quickly to our places where our boots sat with heavy pants tucked down around them. We kicked our shoes off and stepped into the boots, pulling the suspenders up over our shoulders as we did. I climbed to my place in the backward-facing seat behind the captain even as I was pulling the soft Nomex fire-resistant hood over my head and shoulders. Next came my coat with the snaps running down the front. I was fumbling with my safety belt when I felt the truck starting to roll. We turned left and the big Cummins Diesel, under the cover beside me, suddenly roared to a crescendo as Don's foot pushed it to full power. The acceleration almost tossed me from my seat before I finally managed to snap the buckle. Then came the heavy helmet.

The fire engine lurched from side to side and front to back as Don wove through the heavy evening traffic at unbelievable speed. Its siren and blasting air horn rattled windows and echoed back to us from buildings we passed. I caught a glimpse of our rapidly flashing reflection in the front windows of a store. I saw faces staring at us from the sidewalks and cars we passed. I couldn't help smiling to myself when I thought I could see looks of awed respect on some of the faces. A real feeling of pride rose in my chest as I watched those ordinary people we left behind. Suddenly, I knew I was different. I was doing something they could never do. I was a firefighter, and I was on my way to face the dragon and extinguish its breath.

We sat in positions dictated by our tasks. Don was at the steering wheel with the captain beside him. Luis was nozzleman, and he sat facing backward in the bucket seat behind Don. I was designated as hydrant man and sat behind the captain on the curb side of the bucket. The engine cover was between Luis and me, and a partition with a sliding window separated the bucket from the cab.

I reviewed in my head the steps I had to take as hydrant man. No time for a foul-up now. This was the real thing! My heart pounded harder.

Suddenly the siren quit and the Engine pulled to a quick stop in front of a dirty white building. I heard the captain speaking into his microphone, "Dispatch—Engine Five on the scene. We have a fifty by fifty-foot masonry single-story building. Nothing showing. Engine Five will investigate; other units stage one block away."

Where was the hydrant? Why hadn't we stopped beside a hydrant so I could hook a hose to supply the engine's pump with water? The answer hit me then. Of course. The captain thought it was just a small fire. He was planning to use water from our on-board water tank. I saw Luis stepping down from the other side of the Engine so I bailed out and dashed around to the compartment where our breathing apparatus was stored. Jerking it open, I pulled mine out and threw it over my head, catching the straps on my shoulders as the tank fell behind my back. I yanked the harness tight, threw my helmet back off my head, pulled the mask into place and was refastening the helmet chinstrap when a suffocating feeling told me I'd forgotten to turn on the air tank's valve.

I looked around, puzzled. Luis and the captain were nowhere to be seen. I couldn't figure out how they could possibly have gotten their breathing gear on so fast. Don was standing, arms folded, near the front of the Engine. I reached up and grabbed a couple of loops of hose on the Mattydale lay—a load of one-and-a-half-inch hose laid crossways of the truck for easy access from either side—and pulled all 150 feet of it off and onto the sidewalk. I found the nozzle and took off running for the front door of the restaurant.

I charged inside and continued on through the dining room to the kitchen doors. Bursting through them, I came to an abrupt stop. There stood Luis and Captain Meaker with several waitresses and cooks looking at the mess made when the fire extinguishers over the fat fryers had done their job. There was no fire left for me and my hose.

The captain and Luis heard the commotion and turned around. They both looked once and then again. Their faces mirrored disbelief. Luis began to smile a big cat and canary smile and the captain raised both hands to his face and hid his eyes for several seconds. The man I took to be the owner stood beside him with a puzzled expression. When the captain finally took his hands from his face he was smiling, too. Turning to the man in the cook's white suit he said, "It's his first fire. Too bad it wasn't bigger, he's all ready!"

And me? I just stood there listening to the air whistling in and out of my mask as I breathed. I was kind of glad I was wearing the mask.

. . . .

Don backed the engine into its bay so easily I figured he could probably do it without looking. We climbed down and set our gear for the next time. I was feeling absolutely ashamed of myself as I turned and started toward the day room. I hadn't gone far when I was surrounded by a gang of little kids. All shades of brown and black, they were clamoring for Luis.

I turned to look for him and spotted him coming out of the bunk room hall with a couple of books in his hand. The kids smiled and chattered as Luis led them to the front lawn where they sat in a circle around him as he found his place in *Bambi* and began reading. Captain Meaker and Don went out to join the circle. I stayed inside and did the dishes like a good little Booter while I listened through the open window and felt sorry for myself.

Luis read for about twenty minutes in a voice that seemed to be acting out the story. The kids listened, looking enthralled, as flames from the forest fire chased the fleeing animals. Just before Luis finished, the captain left for a moment and came back with a basketful of small paper bags. He handed one to each child and told them to take them home. "Tomatoes from the garden out back," he answered my questioning eyes. "We got a little carried away when we planted them."

It was getting dark by then and all but four of the kids left. Luis led the quartet into the day room and sat on the couch with them. "They don't speak English, yet," he explained. "Took a little doing, but I finally found *Bambi* in the Spanish section of the library." He started reading, his voice taking the parts of the characters again, but in a different language. I had been looking forward to a good movie on television that night and missing it so someone could read stories to dirty-faced little Mexican kids didn't help my disposition much. I went out and sat on the front porch. I could hear Luis's voice through the window. Behind the station I could hear Captain Meaker and Don playing basketball with five or six black teenagers. I watched the low riders cruising past and laughed at them inside.

. . . .

A little later we had another run to a minor auto accident. We were just getting ready to turn in when the tones came again. The voice from the speakers said, "A first alarm assignment. Twenty fourth and State Street—Twenty fourth and State Street. Fire reported in an abandoned manufacturing plant. Engine Six, Engine Five, Engine Nineteen, Engine Twenty-two. Ladder Six, Ladder Twenty-two, Utility One, Battalion Three. Use channel one."

I knew the dispatcher's computer had shown this location to be a large building. She was calling for more equipment than an ordinary fire would require. She called the companies out in the order they were due to arrive at the scene. We were the second-due Engine.

There was very little traffic that late at night, but Don still used the siren and blasted the air horn at every intersection. And when, at one intersection, we narrowly missed a pickup truck that came banging through on a yellow light, I understood why. We hadn't gone far when I heard another voice from the radio speaker behind my head. "Engine Six on the scene. We have a five story masonry, one hundred by one hundred-and-fifty feet. Fire showing on the second floor, east side. Engine Five take a line to second floor. Exposure is a three story frame dwelling ten feet from fire. Exposure is hot. Engine Six will take the exposure. Engine Nineteen supply Engine Five. Engine Twenty-two stage one block south. Ladder Six take ventilation. Ladder Twenty-two handle search and rescue. Engine Six is passing command to Battalion Three."

I tensed up. It was a working fire in a large building with another building exposed to danger from the flames. We were to go straight in without taking a hydrant and hit the fire with water from our tank while Engine 19 came in behind us with a hose from a hydrant. Engine 6 would protect the exposed building—after rescue, the first priority is always to protect unburned property. The Engine companies would attack the flames while the Ladders ventilated the burning building of smoke and heat and searched for possible victims. The utility unit would supply fresh air tanks, lights, and other support. The Battalion Chief would take command from the first-in captain as soon as he arrived.

Another voice broke in. It was the Battalion Chief. "Engine Nineteen, Battalion Three. Engine Nineteen lay double hoses. Supply Engine Five then take the third floor to cover fire extension up there."

Engine 19 acknowledged, just as we pulled to a stop in front of the building. Luis and I bailed out. I caught only one quick look upward to where orange flames were rolling from three corner windows as the flames licked the eaves of the house next door. Engine 6 already had water playing on the side of the house and another hose stretched through the front door.

The scene was one of carefully organized chaos as Luis, the captain, and I pulled our breathing apparatus out of the compartment and put it on. Don was twirling handwheels and pulling valve handles to get water from the tank to our hoses. I was aware of Ladder 6 in the street beside us and saw their big aerial ladder starting up over our heads. The men from Ladder 22 headed in the door just as Captain Meaker called, "Pull the two-and-a-half!"

I was ready to go by then, thankful that all my rehearsals at The Grinder had let me keep up with the others. Luis and I walked quickly to the rear of our Engine and pulled down the nozzle and first lengths of the heavy two-and-a-half-inch attack hose. We followed the captain through the front door and up the stairs. Turning right, we moved in a half crouch down the hallway. The captain paused to feel each door we passed and to close any doors that were standing open. I could hear a dull rumble ahead and knew that it was the sound of the fire. Small flashlights, attached to our helmets by strips of innertube, cast an eerie flicker up and down the hall.

We reached the end door in the hall. I could see wisps of smoke puffing out of the top. Captain Meaker spoke into his hand radio, "Engine Five, charge our line." Luis opened the nozzle just a little to flush air from the hose. Suddenly, just as the hose was getting stiff, he handed the nozzle to me, tapped the captain on the helmet and made a choking sign with his hands to indicate that he wasn't getting enough air from his breathing equipment. The captain moved behind him and checked valves and hoses. Then, shaking his head, he motioned for Luis to leave. He spoke quietly into his radio through the speaker port on his mask, "Engine Five, Captain Five. Don, Luis is on his way out. Watch for him."

Luis was just disappearing down the stairs when the captain cracked the door open a little and peered inside. I could see past his helmet to the orange-yellow flames wreathing across the ceiling. They curled down the walls into little whirlpools of fire. Once again I was struck, as I had been in all the training fires, by the savage beauty of the flames. Heat rolled from the room and engulfed us.

The captain closed the door and moved aside to let me into position. As he did, he shouted through the speaker in his air mask, "Wait until I give you the word and then open up. Remember to sweep it from. . . ."

He didn't finish. I shoved the door aside and opened the nozzle. The cone-shaped spray of water poured into the room as I swept the nozzle around from floor to ceiling following the curling path of the flames. It was always fascinating to watch the water beat the fire back, pushing it across the room, snuffing as it chased.

Someone was pounding on my back and yelling in my ear. I looked behind the plastic lens of the captain's mask into his angry eyes. He was yelling, "No! No! Shut it down! Shut it down!"

Puzzled, I shut down the nozzle and watched flames slowly come back into the room. The captain was still shouting into my ear. "I *told* you to wait until I gave you the word! Didn't anyone teach you to listen to your captain?" He jerked the nozzle from my hands and shouldered me out of the way. We crouched there while the fire built again. Then I heard a voice from the radio attached to his coat, "Okay, Engine Five. You can open up now, we're clear." All of a sudden I understood. The captain opened the nozzle and began duckwalking into the hot room behind the cone of water spray, and within seconds the room was dark again.

We were back on the sidewalk pulling off sweat-soaked coats when a tall man wearing a captain's red helmet with a reflective "L22" on the side came up to us. Shouldering his breathing gear, he asked Captain Meaker, "Was it your Booter?"

Captain Meaker nodded silently and motioned toward me.

The ladder captain turned and planted his wagging finger right under my nose. In a low, threatening voice he said, "I hope you know what you did. We were in the hall on the other side of that room searching out the building. When you opened up without an all clear, you drove that fire right down on top of us. We were as flat on the floor as we could get, and the flames were still scorching our underpants." He paused to let that soak in. Then he added in a growl, "If you *ever* do that to us again, I'll personally barbecue you. Do you understand that?"

I nodded meekly while he stood glaring at me, then he turned to stalk back to his ladder truck.

I looked up at the captain. He wasn't smiling, but there was an amused little twist at the corners of his mouth. I'd always made it a point never to apologize to a Black or a Mexican, but now I found myself saying lamely, "I'm sorry."

He nodded and began changing the bottle on his air pack. I set mine down beside his and began changing it. I was just tightening the hose when he put his hand on my shoulder and said quietly, "Y'know, Booter, we all have a need to prove ourselves, and we usually try too hard at first. Take it easy and it'll go better." He tightened the tank clamp on his pack and then added with a grin, "Hey, Booter. The time I did what you just did, I broiled a Bat Chief. Mercy, you got off easy!"

. . . .

We didn't run again that night, but I didn't sleep, either. I just lay rigid in bed waiting for the tones to come again and kicking myself everyplace I could reach.

Chapter Four

I got home from my first shift on duty and found my mother waiting for me at the door. "Did you have breakfast?" was the first thing she asked. The second thing she asked: "Was it exciting?"

We went into the kitchen. I sat at the table while she brewed a big pot of welcome coffee for me. "Would you believe," I asked her, "that they don't have coffee in that place?"

"Why not?" she asked.

"They're all Mormons!" I replied. "Real, live Mormons who think coffee and anything else that normal people like are sins."

She laughed. "Well, you won't go to Mass with your dad and me, maybe they'll do you some good."

"I doubt it," I smiled. Then I started answering her questions about my first day on the new job.

I told her about the runs we'd had. I left out a couple of details, but she hung on every word just like she used to when I'd come home from a high school basketball game. I finished by telling her about Luis reading to the kids and how they all prayed before meals and even how they had knelt in prayer before the day's work started. I shook my head, "They're even more religious than the sisters at St. Stephanie's."

She sat quietly. Then she said in a thoughtful voice, "Maybe you'd better not say too much about that to your father. You know how he feels about Mormons. . . ."

I nodded silently and then got up to call Linda.

. . . .

One of the best side parts of being a firefighter is the forty-eight hours you have off between shifts. Many of us have second jobs or own businesses. I work with my brother-in-law in his auto body shop, now, but back then I had all forty-eight of those lovely hours free.

Linda and I headed into the mountains outside the city. We spent the day walking and just sitting around. She's a quiet girl with long, dark hair and a pretty little Irish button nose. She was attending college to become a Kindergarten teacher. That day she seemed especially quiet and serious as I told her about my first day's adventures.

I could tell something was eating at her, so I held her close and asked what it was. She shook her head the first time I asked, but the second time she replied, "I don't know. . . I guess I'm just a little worried."

"About what?"

"About you," she smiled up at me. "You and all that fire and smoke. Firemen get killed, you know."

"Yeah, but so do traveling salesmen."

"Yes," she answered, "but maybe they don't die such horrible deaths."

I didn't have an answer to that one, so I just stopped talking. So did she, until a few minutes later when she started talking about plans for the wedding.

. . . .

I met death for the first time on the next shift.

. . . .

Captain Meaker offered the prayer in the circle that morning. I joined them again, reluctantly, because I couldn't for the life of me find a nice way to tell them I wasn't interested in their quaint Mormon customs.

He had just finished when the tones came through the speaker, and the voice said, "Engine Five, Engine Twenty-two, Ladder Twenty-two, Battalion Three. A drowning. A drowning in the canal south of 22nd at Iverson. The canal south of 22nd at Iverson. Use channel one."

We didn't pull on our firefighting clothes. We wouldn't need them. I tossed my boots and pants into the bucket beside my coat and helmet and scrambled in after them. Iverson was only about a block and a half away. We rolled up and found a small crowd of excited black and brown people along the canal bank where water fed under the freeway through a long, concrete tunnel. One of them, a small woman wearing the heavy make-up and sleazy-thin, skin-hugging slit skirt I mark a prostitute by, was screaming at us as we piled off. "He in th' tunnel! He in th' tunnel!"

Luis came around the back of the Engine with a coil of rope over his shoulder. Don followed him with another. The captain had the woman by the shoulders, trying to shake answers from her, but she just kept screaming at him. "You gotta get 'im, Man! You jist gonna stan' there an' let 'im drowned. Man, he my little boy an' he be down in that tunnel! Don' jist stan' here, for God's sake, do s'thin' . . . do s'thin'! You's a fireman. . . do s'thin'!"

A little Mexican boy stepped up to Luis. "Luis! Hey, man! It's Butcher. . . he an' us was walkin' along here an' fishin' an he slipped in an' the water pull him into that tunnel. We could hear him yellin' inside there but we cou'n't see him."

Luis grabbed the kid by the shoulder. "How long?" he asked. "How long's he been in there?"

"I dunno. . . maybe ten, fifteen minutes. Half hour, maybe. I hadda run down an' call from th' store."

"You sure he didn't come out the other end?"

"He couldn't. There's that big pile of junk they never cleaned out before water came this summer!"

Luis threw the coil of rope to the ground and began to pull off his shirt and kick his shoes off. "Strip, Booter!" he shouted to me as he unbuckled his pants and let them drop to the ground. To the captain he shouted, "It's little Butcher. He's been in there half an hour!"

I still stood there, staring at Luis and his strange underwear while he tied a knot in the rope around his waist. "Dammit, Booter, strip!" he shouted again.

Captain Meaker seemed to be thinking as he looked at the water pouring into the concrete opening. Then he turned to me. "How good a swimmer are you?"

"I SCUBA dive."

"Can you handle it in there?"

"I think so."

"Then get stripped and rope up. Go in with Luis while we tend the ropes." The calmness of his voice surprised me.

I looked at the crowd around us and hesitated. There was something about taking my clothes off in front of a crowd. . . . Then I looked up at Luis. His eyes were boring through me while he waited, ready to go. "Booter," the captain said, with an edge in his otherwise quiet voice, "we know this one. He's one of the kids who hang out at the station. He's only eleven years old." Then he added in almost a whisper, "I can't help much. I'm not a very good swimmer."

That surprised me, somehow, and galvanized me into action. I stripped to my undershorts and didn't think another thing of it. I secured the rope with a bowline on a bight around my waist and chest and followed Luis down the slippery cement bank to the rushing water. The water was warm enough, but the current pulled and tugged at me as my feet entered it. My legs were grabbed and swept from under me. Then I was in the water struggling to hold my head above it as the rope's pull tried to force my head under.

I looked up straight into the morning sun. I could see the captain silhouetted against the brightness, holding the other end of my rope. Just then a couple of men from Engine 22 showed up and grabbed the rope with him. I felt much better with three men holding me. Luis nodded . . . I couldn't have heard him above the rush of the water. He waved his arm. I felt the rope slacken as they let me drift toward the maw of the tunnel.

I didn't know what to expect as I slid under the highway into sudden blackness. Dirty, brown water poured over and around us; its rush echoed back and forth from rounded walls. Ahead, I could dimly make out an opening of light on the other side of the freeway. Light from behind me lit up Luis' head. There was about a foot of clearance between the water level and the top of the tunnel. Suddenly it hit me that water level in the canals could change in a couple of minutes as demand for irrigation water changed—that at any time the tunnel could fill completely leaving no place for us.

The water pulled us along. Ahead, I could see the outlines of a jam of wood, tires, branches, and other debris. I looked back, straight into the beam of a powerful spotlight. Beside the spot I could make out a man hanging from a ladder suspended from the top of the tunnel: another firefighter, keeping an eye on us and relaying signals to the men on shore who held our ropes—and lives—in their hands. That sight made me feel better. But not much.

I slammed into the piled debris so hard it hurt. I could see Luis sweeping his arms and feet around the pile's tangled surface. I swept my left foot out and immediately found something soft and yielding. I followed my leg with my hand and felt cold, wet skin. I shivered and tried to grab something but my hand kept slipping off.

I couldn't make Luis hear me above the noise of the water, so I kicked him. He looked around the second time I kicked, and I motioned downward into the water. He struggled over to me. I reached under with both hands, ducking my head, and grabbed two hands full of hair. I pulled. Nothing moved. My hands slipped again.

Luis ducked under and stayed down for a long time. When he surfaced, he handed me part of a rope and motioned for me to help him pull. We pulled, bracing ourselves against the jam. Suddenly the rope gave. The boy's coiled black hair bobbed up in front of me. I slid my arms under his and around his chest while Luis threw a loop of rope around both the boy and me. I saw him wave to the men at the tunnel opening. The rope around my body became tight.

Water kept breaking over my head as the men pulled me against the current. At times I went without air for what seemed an awfully long time. Then, with a rush, the ladder swept past backward, and I swam into dazzling light.

Hands pulled and tugged me, and the burden I carried, up another ladder sloping along the smooth cement canal wall. The rope that bound the boy to me was untied. Hands pulled him away and laid him on a blanket. A circle of men gathered. I could see the captain's head bobbing up and down over the boy's face as he breathed into him while another man in a police uniform pumped on his chest.

They counted. "One, one thousand; two, one thousand; three, one thousand. . ." The monotonous rhythm of men fighting for a life. I sat on the ground beside Luis, gasping air and energy back into me. Then I stood up and walked past Luis to stand behind the circle of men who knelt around the boy. A large, silent Black man picked up a blanket from the tailboard of Engine 5 and gently wrapped it around my shoulders. I looked at him in surprise and nodded genuine thanks to him. I was suddenly very cold.

Off to one side the thin-clad prostitute cried quietly in the arms of an older, fat Black woman.

The crowd of firemen shifted as the captain and the policeman traded places with two other men in uniforms. I could hear Luis whispering something to himself. It sounded like another prayer. The monotony of the rhythm continued as a paramedic rescue unit rolled to a stop beside our Engine. Captain Meaker stood between Luis and me as the paramedics took over.

We all watched. I realized I was holding my breath as a straight line glowed across the tiny screen of the paramedics' monitor. Twice they shocked him. Then again. But still the line remained flat. The monotonous counting stopped. One of the paramedics shook his head. The other spoke into his radio. "Three tries and no conversion. Still a straight line."

From the radio I heard another voice, hollow and far away, "Ten-four, Rescue Twelve. Might as well call it."

Off to one side, I heard the Black woman-of-the-night stifling a cry.

. . . .

We cleaned the Engine and sorted its equipment in silence that morning. I couldn't get the little boy out of my mind. I could feel his coldness against my chest. And yet I didn't really feel much emotion. Just an emptiness.

No one offered any praise to Luis or me for what we'd done that morning. It was just part of the job. It was expected.

Later in the evening, while sitting on the front porch beside the captain, and while Luis read to the children again, I ventured an observation I'd been feeling all day. "He's probably better off dead."

Captain Meaker raised his eyebrows. "What?" he asked.

"That kid. He's probably better off dead than growing up down here with a whore for a mother."

The captain didn't say anything for a long time. Then he stood up and said, "Booter, you still have a lot to learn."

He turned and walked into the kitchen where I heard him open a pop bottle; Luis kept reading.

Chapter Five

A bunch of us from my Academy class met at Dudley's one evening, on our off shifts, to soak up a few beers and swap tales. My classmates were all trying to top one another, but whenever they turned to me for a story, I couldn't seem to come up with much. Dave Rogers, trying to get something out of me, asked about the day in the tunnel under the freeway. I told them, but there wasn't much enthusiasm in it. I couldn't understand why thoughts of a small Black kid I'd never even met left me feeling so empty inside.

We were on about the second round when who should walk in but most of the training staff? Chief Clark led the way directly to our table. "So, they haven't got rid of the bunch of ya yet? Must be we taught 'em good."

The other trainers laughed. Captain Kojwalski added, "We sure do good work!"

They sat down with us, and we bought them another round. We had to go back through the recitations of our experiences again for them, though I still kept quiet. Finally, Kojwalski turned to me. "Well, I heard some good things about you. That rescue under the freeway was a little hairy, wasn't it?"

"It wasn't a rescue!" I answered, surprised at the anger in my voice. "The kid died!"

Captain Kojwalski laughed. "Inconsiderate kid! And after you risked your tail for him, too." But then he looked at me and added in a softer tone, "You'll learn soon enough, Boot, that it's not at all like T. V. *They* save 'em all. A lot of *ours* die."

The subject changed quickly when Chief Clark asked me, "What do you think of the Mormon Batallion?"

Captain Burke laughed, "Yeah, Booter. Have they got you yet?"

I shook my head ruefully and Chief Clark laughed again. "Y'better watch it, Booter. Those people are out to convert the world. They'll be working on you pretty soon. You must look like good meat to them. Yep, if you don't watch it, we'll soon be calling you Brother Bootie and you'll have five wives and twenty kids!" The rest of them laughed loudly.

When the laughing settled down, Danny Pingree, another of my classmates, looked puzzled. "Hey," he said, "I thought you said your captain is a Black?"

"He is," I confirmed.

"Then how can he be a Mormon? They don't let Blacks into their church. It's just for the lily-white—they figure they're the only ones who'll get into Heaven, and they wouldn't want it cluttered up with any Black folks, would they?"

I just shook my head. I didn't know. But since he'd mentioned it, I recalled hearing that Mormons weren't too friendly to Black people. I found myself thinking that in one thing, at least, the Mormons had good sense.

I drove home later with a troubled mind. I knew that Mormons like to try to convert everyone in sight to their way of thinking, and after all I'd heard my father say about the Mormons with their golden Bible and strange, secret ways, I wanted nothing to do with them, either.

I headed straight for home and waited nervously until Dad got in from work. Then I popped it on him. He sat still for a few moments, then he stood up. "Y'know what I'd do if I was you?" he asked. Without giving me a chance to respond, he went on. "I'd be real careful until I could arrange me a transfer into another station. That's what I'd do."

He disappeared for a few moments and I could hear him rummaging around in his bedroom. When he came back, he was carrying a small, blue book. "Here, read this," he commanded. "It explains all about them devils."

I opened the book to its introduction. It was called *The Mormon Church Exposed*. It had been written, the cover stated, by a Protestant minister. I sat down and started to read. The more I read, the more certain I was that I had to get out of Station 5.

But, at the same time, I was puzzled. If all that little book said was true, why hadn't any of the men at the station put a move on me yet? After all, I'd been with them for six shifts. Then I decided they were just biding their time, waiting for the right moment to work their black magic on me—to trap another soul.

I decided to apply for a transfer as soon as I could.

. . . .

The next shift started just like all the others. Again they invited me to kneel with them in prayer. I did since I still couldn't think of a good way out of it. They'd been talking, earlier, about the little boy's funeral, and I knew they'd all gone to it. Luis offered the prayer and it was mostly about the little kid they called "Butcher." It was also filled with remarks about the kid's mother. I found myself thinking sarcastically that Luis was wasting his breath praying for a woman like that. I may not have been as religious as my mother wanted me to be, but she *had* taught me about sin—and that gal was a sinner if I'd ever seen one!

We spent the morning in the back parking lot, checking hose. We attached the hose to our pump, filled it with water, closed the nozzle and ran it up to 300 pounds pressure. We were interrupted once by a run to a shopping center parking lot where gasoline was leaking from a car with a punctured gas tank.

The afternoon took us to a little daycare center in the basement of a place called "The African Reformed First Baptist Church." There must have been about fifty little black and brown kids all jumping up and down and squealing as we pulled into the dirt parking lot beside the run-down little white building. I climbed from the Engine and was immediately surrounded by a flock of them. They stopped bouncing and squealing and just stood, staring up at me.

Captain Meaker gathered the group around the front of the Engine and began talking to them. "How many of you were here the last time we came?" he asked.

A bunch of little hands went up.

"Okay," he asked. "Who remembers what you should never do with fire?"

He pointed to one jet-black boy who shyly raised his hand. "Play with it!" the little guy answered.

"Right! Now, what do you do if you need to get help fast, like if there's a house on fire on your street?"

"Get a grown-up to call nine-one-one," answered a little girl whose giggle made me smile in spite of myself.

Captain Meaker kept asking questions, the kids kept answering. I was surprised at how much they knew. I hadn't thought these Blacks who lived south of the freeway were intelligent enough to learn things like that, especially so young.

When the questions were finished we went inside, down into the church's cool, musty basement where we let each kid put on our turnout coats and helmets. Luis helped a couple of them try out his breathing apparatus, then we taught them how to stop, drop, and roll if their clothing ever caught fire.

There was one little brown boy, about four years old, who never said a word. He just sat, staring at me. At first, it made me feel uncomfortable. Then I tried smiling at him. His eyes lit up and a little smile turned the corners of his mouth. Soon I was making faces at him, and he was silently giggling.

When we'd finished indoors, we went back to the parking lot and showed the kids the insides of Engine 5. Finally, Captain Meaker announced that it was time for the biggest treat of all. "Who has been the quietest kid here?" he asked. Then he pointed toward me. "He's our newest fireman. We call him Booter. Shall we let Booter decide who's been quietest and who's listened best?"

The kids shouted agreement. As I looked over their faces, I spotted the little brown boy. He was looking at me with pure pleading in his eyes so I pointed to him. Captain Meaker nodded. He asked, "What's your name?"

We had to listen closely, three times, before we understood. "David," he whispered.

"Well, David," the captain grinned, "we always let the quietest kid make the biggest noise. Booter, why don't you take David up in the cab and let him blow the siren?"

I boosted the little guy into the cab. I stood on the step beside him and showed him how to switch the electronic siren through its full range of noises. Then I let him step on the foot switch that controls the Traffic Blaster air horn. He loved it! I was enjoying it, too. So much that I let him keep blasting until the captain tapped me on the shoulder and drew his fingers across his throat to tell me to quit.

I set David back on the ground and was just turning around when I heard our tones on the radio. The dispatcher's voice followed. "Engine Five, Engine Six, Ladder Six, Utility One. Third alarm assignment. 46th Street and Wilberry. 46th Street and Wilberry. Third alarm equipment stage at the railroad crossing south on Wilberry. Use channel three."

We started jumping into our protective clothing while the crowd of kids watched with delight. I was heading around the back of the Engine when one of the women caring for the children grasped my sleeve. She was a big lady with dark black skin and concern in her eyes. "Y'all be keerful, now," she said. Then she added, "And God bless ya!"

I nodded and kept going. I climbed into my seat and fastened my safety belt just as Don started rolling the big red truck. As we began to move, I caught a glimpse of David holding the big woman's hand. He waved to me as we turned onto the street, and I waved back.

. . . .

While we were still a couple of miles from 46th and Wilberry I could see a huge cloud of black smoke looming up. I knew it was a warehouse district and figured we'd be in for a big fight when we got there. My adrenalin was pumping as we approached. I heard a voice from the speaker behind my head announce, "Engine Five, Divison One. Engine Five lay doubles from the hydrant one block south on Wilberry. Take the southeast corner with your monitor and supply another line to Engine One sixty-three. Engine Six, Division One. Lay from the hydrant at the alley east of Wilberry behind the Continental Bakery and get on the bakery roof. A lot of embers are landing up there. Cover the exposure."

We pulled up, finally, beside the hydrant the Division Chief had told us to take. Luis and I pulled two of the two-and-a-half-inch hoses from our bed and connected them to the hydrant. I waited there while Don drove Engine 5 slowly down the street laying double lines behind the Engine to the corner of the building. I waited until I saw Don signal then I cranked the wrench on the top of the hydrant and turned water into our hoses.

By the time I got up to the Engine, the captain and Luis had already laid a line to Engine 163 so we could supply it with more water. I climbed on top of the Engine and swung the nozzle of our big turret gun, or monitor, around until it pointed toward the flaming building. Don turned a valve. Water began to pour from the monitor's nozzle.

The entire roof of the huge warehouse was ablaze. I began to sweep water from our gun back and forth across it. Water quenched the fire only until the stream moved on, then the fire flashed right back up. I looked to my right and left. All up and down both streets fire engines and ladder trucks were pouring water onto the fire. There must have been five miles of hose on the street. I found myself dreading the clean-up after this mess.

We were about a hundred feet from the building, but heat was still intense up where I was. Engine 163 was a lot closer with its monitor also trained on the roof. One of their men was sitting on the end of a two-and-a-half-inch hose on the sidewalk pouring water through a window onto flames inside. I directed the stream from our gun over so spray from it would fall back on 163. Men on top of the Engine waved their thanks. The man on the sidewalk gave me a thumbs-up sign. I recognized him, then, as Danny Pingree.

I looked back at the building and was startled to notice a crack in the cement block wall that hadn't been there a moment before. Then I saw that the wall was starting to lean slightly outward. I reached down, whacked Don on the helmet and pointed to the wall. He nodded and picked up his radio microphone. I heard his voice in the speaker. "Division One, Engine Five. We have crack in the southeast corner wall. The wall's going to go."

Don moved to the cab and reached inside. There was a short blast on the siren then I saw him pointing toward the wall, warning the men on 163. They looked toward the wall and waved to indicate they'd seen it. Danny shut down his nozzle and was just getting up when I saw the wall starting to roll outward. Danny had his back to it and didn't see it coming. I shouted, but the roar of our engine drowned out my voice. I watched in frozen horror as the wall peeled out and downward, right on top of Danny.

There was a loud *whump* as the blocks hit the sidewalk. A huge burst of flame and sparks enveloped the whole front of Engine 163. When it subsided, there was only a pile of broken brick and flaming roof wood where Danny had been.

I sat, stunned. Suddenly Don was beside me shouting into my ear, "Get water on him! Get water on him! He's down in there and he'll broil if you don't wet it down!" I swung the stream around and watched while Don jumped down and ran to join Luis, the captain, and the other men from Engine 163 as they began digging frantically through the pile with their gloved hands.

I heard another voice, shouting, on the radio. "We've got a man under the wall on the southwest—no, no, the south*east* side. Get us some help!"

Men came running from everywhere. Three turret guns were turned on the fire in that corner trying to beat the flames back. Still, you could see the men gathered there trying to shield themselves from its heat despite water from my gun playing directly on them.

They dug for what seemed an awfully long time, then I saw them lifting a form in fire clothes from the ruins. The normally yellow fire coat was scorched brown. They carried Danny behind 163 to where I couldn't see any more. I kept my nozzle on the fire until long after the ambulance had gone.

. . . .

The telephone was ringing when we finally got back to Station 5. Don answered and called me. "It's your mother. She's worried about you."

I took the phone, feeling a little angry. "Mom," I exploded. "You don't need to call down here. I'm okay."

Her voice seemed far away. "I wasn't sure," she said plaintively. "I saw it on television and I could see your fire truck right there. They didn't give the name of the man who was hurt, and I've been waiting all afternoon for the phone to ring. I kept calling your station and no one would answer!"

"Well, I'm okay!" I answered tartly. "And please don't go calling down here every time you think you need to check on me. I'll be all right! I'm not a little boy any more!" With that, I hung up the phone.

I turned and found Captain Meaker standing there beside me. "Boot," he said firmly, "there was absolutely no call for that. Your mother has every right in the world to worry about you. You're in the most dangerous job in the country, you know that! We're all going to call our wives to let them know we're okay. Then I think you'd better call her back and apologize."

They all called home. Captain Meaker called last. When he finished, he handed me the phone. I could tell by the look on his face that there was no way out of it. I called my mother and apologized. But it angered me to have someone else, especially a Black someone else, prowling around in my private affairs.

Then the captain called dispatch and asked about Danny. He turned to us after he hung up. "They've got him in the burn unit. He's apparently not as bad off as we thought he was." He paused, "Maybe we ought to have a word of prayer for him before we get supper."

We knelt again and the captain offered a long prayer. I wondered what Danny would think if he knew he had a bunch of Mormons saying prayers for him.

. . . .

Nobody felt much like cooking that night, so we climbed aboard Engine 5 and drove around the corner to the Kentucky Fried Chicken place.

Chapter Six

I worried about Danny Pingree all that night. After I got off the next morning, I drove to Station One and wandered into the department offices to see how he was doing. I wasn't the only one visiting the personnel office that morning. Several firefighters I didn't know were there ahead of me. I walked in just in time to hear one of the secretaries saying, "He's still in the burn unit, but they've taken him off the critical list. He has a couple of broken ribs and his back and legs have first and second-degree burns. But somebody got water on him quickly enough to save him from worse."

I walked out without speaking to anyone and headed for home. My mother and father were still at the breakfast table when I got there, so I joined them.

"You're late this morning," was the first thing my mother said.

"Yeah, I stopped off at Station One to see how Danny Pingree's doing. He's the man who was hurt yesterday."

"How is he?" my father asked.

"Okay. We got water on him fast enough so he didn't get burned too badly."

My mother's face wore a worried expression. "Do burning buildings cave in very often?"

I nodded. "Yes, it's a real hazard. In fact, some buildings are designed to cave in when they burn. Y'know those wide spanned, balloon roofs you see on a lot of supermarkets and places like that? Well, they figure its cheaper to build them so they'll cave in during a fire. Then all they have to do is scoop out debris from between walls left standing and plunk a new roof on top."

"But doesn't that endanger firemen who have to fight fires in there?"

"Yep, it sure does. But what's a few firemen here and there? They can always find new ones. Architects and engineers don't think of firefighters. All they've got on their minds is dollars." Mom was looking so worried by then that I added, "But we know about the hazard, so we don't stay in places like that when a really hot fire has been burning for any length of time. Our officers will pull us out and let the building go if they think there's danger."

My father was scowling. "So you're gonna trust yourself to that nigger captain?"

I shrugged. "People say he's a good captain," I defended lamely.

My father growled, "No way I'd trust one of them jungle bunnies. When you gonna put in for a transfer?"

I knew better than to argue. My dad's been a truck driver all his life, and I learned a long time ago that you don't argue with a truck driver. Besides, I was pretty sure he was right.

"I'll call the Bat Chief on the next shift," I said.

"Call the *what?*" my mother asked.

I laughed. "The Bat Chief," I explained. "The Battalion Chief."

"Oh," she nodded.

. . . .

Linda was late leaving the university that afternoon. She was busy getting a pile of stuff ready to start student teaching in January. I met her near the library. We drove up to the skyline road to a place we liked to sit and talk. Spread out below us, the city was like a map. As the sun slipped down behind us, I could see the shadow of the mountain, where we sat, spreading across buildings and streets. Lights began to flick on here and there.

We talked about lots of things. Linda's school. The wedding in December. We planned a trip to start looking for an apartment. Then I brought up the idea of transferring from Station 5.

Linda brushed some of her long hair back along her shoulder. "Why would you want to do that? I thought you said you'd like it because it's a busy station."

"It is, but I feel funny working with a Mexican and a nigger."

"Black. . ., not nigger," she chided me.

"Besides, you know they're all Mormons. I keep waiting for them to put some moves on me. You know what they say about Mormons—how they're always trying to convert the whole world. I kind of like being Catholic."

Linda was quiet for a few moments. "Why?" she asked. "You absolutely refuse to go to Mass. You know the only reason you agreed to a church wedding was to satisfy your mother and mine. How can you be a satisfied Catholic if you don't take part?"

"I just am," I replied. "I grew up that way. I don't see any reason to change now."

The lights below were taking over the night. We watched in silence for a while before Linda spoke again. "I know some Mormons, too, and they've never tried to push me into anything. In fact, I kind of admire them sometimes."

I sat up. "You do?"

"Yes. They seem to have something I don't. I don't know what, exactly. Maybe it's just that they seem to *believe* in what they believe. Sometimes I feel as if I don't know what I believe. I'm not even sure I know what the church believes when I read of all the disputes and arguments between the Vatican and the clergy and between the clergy and the lay members. It's almost as though the rock the church is supposed to be built upon is crumbling. I wish I had something more solid to stand on."

I didn't say anything, but inside I realized that was the way I felt, too. And that feeling was the reason I had slipped out of the church since I'd left the cloistered halls of junior high school at St. Stephanie's.

It grew darker as we watched the city below us. Linda startled me a little when she broke into my thoughts. "Did you know him?"

"Know who?"

"The fireman who got hurt yesterday."

"Oh. Yeah, it was Danny Pingree. He went to the Academy with me. You met him at the graduation."

"I don't remember him."

"Tall, skinny guy with black hair. The one who hardly ever smiles."

"Oh, him. How is he doing?"

"Okay. I saw the wall fall on him and put water on him right away. They dug him out pretty fast, so except for some broken ribs and a few burns, he's okay."

She laid her head against my shoulder. "I still worry about you. I wish you'd find something safer to do."

I laughed. "Heck, firefighting's safer than teaching Kindergarten."

She smiled, but didn't say anything.

We watched the lights as the night grew colder. I was thinking long thoughts when I saw flashing red lights running up a street. A moment later I heard sirens and traffic blasters. Station Twelve was rolling. A prickle ran up my spine. Somehow I knew I couldn't change to something safer.

I knew I'd heard the siren's call.

Chapter Seven

Things had been unusually quiet for several weeks that late summer. Summer bakes the barren streets and their crowded little houses all day and night brings breezeless, stifling heat that seems to suck the breath from anyplace not air conditioned. People of the South Valley stew in the heat and erupt at nights. Fridays and Saturdays, after hours of suffocating boredom, are the worst. In all station houses south of the freeway, on those nights, men on duty become slaves to the dispatcher's tones.

My next shift was a Friday. We stayed busy all day with a rash of automobile accidents. It didn't take long, working as firefighters, for us to become firm believers in using a car's safety belts. We responded to a couple of automobile accidents on every normal shift. It's routine in almost any station in the city.

Ladder trucks normally respond to auto accidents because they carry light rescue equipment—hydraulic cutters and rams, cutting saws and torches—the things needed to pull someone from a mangled mess of steel. But Engine companies respond on a lot of accidents, too.

Within the first two months I was on duty, I'd seen several people horribly injured who probably wouldn't have had a scratch if they'd been wearing safety belts. They ranged from a woman—a back seat passenger—who'd been scalped by the rearview mirror when she flew forward and hit the windshield, to a man half ejected through a sprung door during a roll-over. The car kept rolling and the door cut him neatly in half. Damage to the car was minimal—a couple of hundred dollars worth of dent-banging and some paint would have had it going again.

A couple of accidents really got to me, though. One was a pretty teenaged girl whose head had gone part way through the windshield. She'd been riding in an older car—one of those with elastic material sandwiched between two sheets of glass, to prevent shattering. The hole where her head had punched had closed back down on her and a jagged ring of glass slashed into her face.

She'd regained consciousness before we got there, and we found her thrashing around, trying to pull her head from its trap. The glass cut deeper and deeper as she struggled. Luis and the captain pulled their pocketknives out and began cutting the elastic between the cracks in the glass. They cut as gingerly as they could, but she still screamed and struggled. And as she screamed and struggled, the cruel glass cut deeper and wider despite the efforts of a police sergeant and me as we tried to hold her still.

Happily, she finally lost consciousness again and stopped thrashing around. I don't imagine she's as pretty now as she once was.

Another morning a young mother rammed the back of a truck that had stopped at a traffic light. Her little girl—a little blonde about three or so—had been standing on the front seat when they hit the truck. The cops figured the speed at impact was less than fifteen miles an hour, but the sudden stop tossed the little girl against the dashboard with such force that one of the radio knobs punched a neat, round hole deep into the front of her skull. It depressed the skull by nearly an inch. She lived, but I heard later that the doctors expect the brain damage to be permanent.

Then there was the old man who was riding in the back seat of his grandson's car. They'd been forced off the road at an intersection when someone ran a red light. They smacked a utility pole at about twenty-five miles an hour. The old man smacked the back of the front seat at about the same speed. Broken ribs punctured a lung and I thought he was going to drown on his own blood before the paramedics stabilized him and got him out of there. I never did hear how he turned out.

I soon learned exactly what newspaper reporters mean when they write so politely about "massive head" or "massive chest" injuries.

I'd heard the stories all my life—the excuses for not wearing safety belts. But it didn't take long for me to decide that no matter what, I'd take my chances with a belt around me. Captain Meaker told me that in more than 3000 auto accident responses, he'd seen only one person hurt because of a belt—and she'd been wearing hers loose instead of snugged up.

I've come to the firm belief that anyone who doesn't buckle in as soon as they slide into a car is just an idiot—and that anyone who doesn't fasten a child down is little more than a murderer waiting to commit the crime.

Somebody told me that firefighters are an opinionated lot. I guess we must be. But then I remember that we see things every day that other people are lucky enough not to see. I wonder if we know something they don't know? . . .

. . . .

We had been out on the freeway all afternoon on one of the first Fridays of my career. We'd cut the body of a truck driver from his mangled cab. We hadn't finished supper when the tones hit. "Engine Five, Engine Twenty-two, Ladder Twenty-two, Battalion Three. Structure fire at 1313 South LaVista. 1313 South LaVista. Use channel two."

We were out the doors in less than thirty seconds. As we turned left onto Dyer, I could see an orange glow in the northeast sky. Don wove the Engine through heavy evening traffic and whipped us around the corner onto LaVista where an abandoned house stood wrapped in flames. "They're getting an early start tonight!" Luis yelled over the engine's roar.

Captain Meaker stuck his head through the opening in the window that separated the cab from the bucket seats. "We'll use tank water!" he hollered. I nodded to show him I'd heard. My heart was pounding. This was my first chance to really show my stuff. It was a simple fire, but it would be hot—mighty hot. And even though the countless abandoned houses that litter the valley aren't really worth anything, it *is* considered bad form to let them burn down completely. Besides, every once in awhile there's a wino or someone inside when the kids or the pyros light them.

Don slammed us to a stop right in front of the fire. I bailed off to join Luis on the other side of the Engine where our air packs are stored. I had to push my way through a throng of excited little kids, all brown or black, who crowded as close as to the big red machine as they dared. I heard Don winding the pump up as I pulled my face mask into place and covered my head and the exposed parts of my neck and cheeks with my fire-resistant flash hood. Air whistled in and out of my mask as I reached for the regulator and flipped the switch down to the pressure setting.

Those air masks are life itself to us. "SCBA," we call them. Short for Self Contained Breathing Apparatus. They carry a fifteen to thirty-minute supply of air packed into a tank and fed into our lungs through a regulator that pushes a little pressure into the mask. The regulator keeps smoke or other gases from leaking through if there's a bad seal in the face mask. SCBA's have put firefighting a far cry from the old days of leather lungs when firefighters prided themselves in their ability to eat smoke and die like men.

Luis and I moved quickly to the other side of the Engine, pulling on our gloves as we went. "You take the nozzle," I heard Luis shout through his mask as he handed me the business end of the one-and-a-half-inch hose on the Mattydale lay. I took it from him and turned to face the blazing house as he pulled the rest of the hose onto the ground and began feeding it out as we hurried toward the inferno.

Flames were rolling out of all the windows and the front door. The book says you attack a fire from the unburned side, but there wasn't any unburned side here. It was all on fire. "Looks like they got a little carried away with the gasoline," Luis shouted into my ear as we approached the front door. "Head right in and I'll follow you!"

I paused outside for a moment to flush air from the hose and check the fog spray pattern. I could feel intense heat burning against my skin through the clear plastic of my helmet face shield and the plastic bubble of my SCBA mask. The same old feeling of excitement I'd felt on all the burning drills in The Grinder came back into me. I felt its electric charge coursing through me as I shouted to Luis, "Ready?"

He nodded. I moved onto the front porch, opening the nozzle as I went. I could feel Luis's shoulder behind my back, helping me push against the recoil of hose pressure. I swept the stream of water quickly upward and across the ceiling of the porch where flames licked through the open front door. Then moving right into the doorway itself, I crouched halfway down to send water pouring through the door into the rolling orange flames. Sweeping the nozzle around in a clockwise direction to follow that motion, I chased the fire with blackness as I killed it.

Duckwalking, we moved into the house, following red and orange that still licked ahead and around us. A door opened to our right. I moved into it and back out, quickly, leaving blackness and steam behind. Crossing the living room I tripped over an object on the floor, kicked it out of the way and moved on into the kitchen. It blacked down in a moment. Then we moved to a room that opened off the kitchen, killing the fire in there. I looked quickly out to the back porch and saw no fire there so we reversed our route and backed out of the house, snuffing little spots of lingering flame as we retreated.

In the living room, we met two men wearing yellow helmets with L22 on the sides. Truckies—men from a ladder company—searching the house for possible bodies. We moved on out the front door and found the ladder truck captain in his red helmet. One of his men was rigging a lighting unit on the porch. The captain looked up. I cringed as I recognized him as the one who'd blistered my ears for blistering his behind.

Captain Meaker stood there, too. "Good job," he smiled. "Let the boys from E 22 take the mop up then we can help overhaul after you two take a blow."

I handed the nozzle to a man from 22 and followed Luis to the back of the Engine. We pulled our breathing gear and sweat-soaked coats off and sat on the tailboard. Don brought us a couple of oxygen face masks and two cups of Gatorade. We sat there resting, drinking and breathing pure O^2. Kids crowded in close, staring at us with admiring eyes. One of them, a little bolder than the others, spoke up in an accented voice. "Hey, how hot was it in there?"

Luis answered in Spanish and I saw a look of surprise on the boy's face. Luis and the kids talked back and forth for a few minutes in a language I can't understand. When they finished, Luis said quietly, "Y'know, Booter, not long ago I was one of those boys. Used to think firefighters were the greatest people on earth. Never ever missed a fire in the neighborhood. Truth is, I started a few until I got caught." He paused, sucking in a deep breath of oxygen before he pulled the mask off and continued, "Now, I try to tell 'em, 'don't start fires.' Maybe they listen—maybe they don't. But anyway, for some of them, they don't know a Mexican can be anything but a carwash rag man. Maybe, when they find out I'm a fireman, they'll figure they can be, too." He shrugged and stood up. "Maybe give 'em somethin' t' shoot for, anyhow."

I got up and followed him back into the house where we helped the guys from Engine 22 and their brother Ladder company rake through the ashes looking for hot spots. The arson team came and looked the place over. "Did you see Felix here?" one of them asked me.

"Felix? I don't know him."

"You'll get to know him soon enough," Captain Meaker told me. "He's our friendly local pyromaniac. This one had his mark on it. He likes to use *plenty* of gasoline. Then he tries to help us out by pulling hose or something. He even gave the boys from Station Seven an 'All Clear' on an old hotel one night. Told 'em he'd checked it just before the fire and there hadn't been anyone in it." The captain shook his head ruefully. "But we've never nailed him. Can't get anything to stick. Terrible though it may be to say, I hope to heaven he blows himself up some night before he gets one of us."

. . . .

We were just finishing packing the Mattydale back into its bed when a little boy came pedaling madly up the sidewalk and yelled, "Hey, firemens, there's another house on fire down the street!"

I looked up. Sure enough, there went a large orange glow and a huge shower of sparks. Captain Meaker shouted something into his radio. We all piled aboard Engine 5 and rolled a couple of blocks to the next burning house. It was a carbon copy of the first except that some burning wood fell on me and burned my neck, even through my flash hood. Then I made a mistake and grabbed a glowing piece of red-hot water pipe, in what had been the kitchen wall, and scorched my hand through my glove.

Luis and I were crossing the porch on our way out when he poked me with his elbow and motioned toward a thin little Mexican with a small mustache and a scraggly beard. He looked to be about nineteen or twenty. "Meet Felix Mendoza," Luis said simply.

The little guy came up to us, eyes bright with excitement. "Hey, man! That sure was a hot one, huh? But you guys handled him okay. I helped you pull the hose up. Did you see me?"

"Yeah, I see you," Luis growled. Then he pulled his spanner wrench from its place in his pocket and held it under the little one's nose. "And in five seconds, I better not see you no more, got it?"

Felix's eyes mirrored disappointment. "But Luis, I just helping you." he whined.

"Disappear, runt!" Luis shouted, "Or I'll plant this between you ears!"

Felix left in a hurry while I fought down a terrible temptation to turn a stream from the hose on him. Then, in a sudden surge of surprise, I realized that I actually pitied the little beggar.

. . . .

We ran about five or six times before midnight—I tend to lose track on a busy shift. A couple of stabbings, an auto accident with one man almost dead, a car on fire, and a smoke report that turned out to be steam from a dry cleaning plant. We were rousted out of bed a few times, too, and by morning I was tired and sleepy.

Just as **B**-shift was coming on, the telephone rang and I realized I'd never had a chance to call the Bat Chief about the transfer. Next shift, I promised myself.

It was the Bat Chief on the phone. He asked Captain Meaker to double back on a shift, in Engine 22, to cover for their captain. That left Luis without a ride home so he asked me to take him since he lives out on the north side, not too far from my folks' place. I was trapped—I couldn't very well say no to someone I had to share a fire station with.

We rode in silence to the University area where Luis suddenly said, "Hey, Booter. You did pretty good last night."

"Thanks," I muttered.

"It's kinda hard at first," he continued. "But you stick with it and take the dirty details with a smile. Pretty soon you're one of the crew."

I nodded, hoping that would come soon.

Then, for a reason I still don't understand, I asked, "Are all you guys really Mormons?"

Luis glanced at me with a hint of surprise. "Yeah. Why?"

"Just wondered, I guess. What about Captain Meaker? I thought you didn't let niggers into your church."

When the expression on Luis's face changed abruptly I knew I'd said the wrong thing again. He sat there for almost a minute before he spoke again in low, measured tones. "I hope I never, ever, hear you call the Cap a 'nigger' again. You'll never meet a finer man than that one. He'll roast for you if he needs to."

I sat silent, tending to my driving. There's something about what a firefighter means when he uses that word "roast" that sends shivers up my back and curls into my toes.

Luis continued in a moment. "And, yes, Meaker's a Mormon, too. He just can't be a member of our priesthood, that's all. Someday, maybe. . . but not for now."

We finished the rest of the ride in silence. But just as he got ready to leave the car, Luis added, "Remind me sometime, and I'll tell you all about Dave Meaker."

I drove the rest of the way home feeling I still had a lot to learn.

Chapter 8

I spent the next couple of days moping around the house. I felt full of well-scrambled feelings. My father was home between hauls to Los Angeles, and when we were together he seemed never to let a moment pass without giving me more advice about Blacks, Mormons, Mexicans and life in general. Dad was after me constantly to ask for a transfer. He kept grilling me about what I'd learned from the book he'd given me. He warned me that my soul was in danger of landing in the eternal frying pan. He even tried to drag me down to the parish church for a long talk with Father Lambert. But I resisted that idea, and the more I resisted, the angrier he became and the madder I grew. By the time I left home that morning, we had a stomping, slamming, cussing argument going. As I walked out the door, he shouted after me, "Y'know what? I think you're starting to let those Mormon niggers get to you. You don't change your ways, boy, and you can move out of this house! Y'got that? Move out if you don't like it!"

Driving through the South Valley still gave me the chills, although it wasn't as bad as it had been those first few weeks. But that day in particular, I drove down there in a black mood—and that was a day when things really began to change.

Life at Station 5 melted into a routine. We were busy with calls of all kinds from the usual summertime infernoes set by kids and arsonists in abandoned houses that littered the South Valley to a little boy with his hand caught in a toilet. Runs began to flow together until after awhile none seemed to stand out. Days and weeks on duty took on a certain anonymity and very little of what we did seemed spectacular.

Luis still read to the children every evening. Older kids came to play basketball with the hoop that was beside the Diesel fuel pump out back. I played ball occasionally, but generally I wound up listening to Luis read while I washed dishes.

Don, Luis, and the captain all played the guitar quite well and I sort of plunk away at it. I was right about Don. He was an excellent singer and their tastes in music ran along the same lines as mine, so we began to play and sing together on the front porch almost every evening that we were on duty. Some of the station's neighbors would stop by occasionally to listen and sometimes join in. I have to admit I enjoyed those sessions.

Through all that time, though, I think my attitudes were being slowly overhauled by experiences. Funny, when I'd graduated from the Academy, I'd had the feeling that there wasn't much more anyone could teach me. But somewhere down inside I realized I still had a lot to learn about a lot of things. And, I realize now, I was learning despite myself.

I was just walking in the back door from the parking lot when I heard our tones and the speaker's voice saying, "Engine Five, an EMS call. 2320 South Dyer, Apartment 12. 2320 South Dyer, Apartment 12. Woman having difficulty breathing. Engine Five, use channel three."

In our department, like a lot of others around the country, fire engines make the first response on EMS—Emergency Medical Service—calls. The department figures it's good for public relations and a better use of equipment than having us sitting around the station waiting for something to catch fire. I quickly threw my turnout gear aboard the Engine and scrambled on after it. Don, the Captain, and Luis did the same. The crew from C-shift stood and watched us leave before they turned to go home.

The public housing units we call "The Highrise Ghetto" wasn't far. It's a rabbit warren of tall concrete buildings, narrow streets, and crowded parking lots filled with stripped, derelict automobiles. Those public highrise apartments are a firefighter's nightmare—buildings built with nothing but dollars and cents in mind and the few fire-safety features they do contain are generally messed up by people who inhabit the places.

We pulled to a stop in front of one of the concrete towers and were met by the inevitable swarm of small boys. Don took up his guard position on top of the monitor deck where he could see if any of them tried to take something from anyplace on the Engine. The rest of us grabbed oxygen and first aid equipment. Luis and I followed the captain up the sidewalk and down some stairs into a dim, dingy basement hall. The place smelled of stale wine, stale urine, and stale bodies.

Captain Meaker stopped to bang heavily on a door. The banging echoed, empty, up and down the concrete and steel tunnel. We waited. He banged again. This time a muffled voice answered from inside, "Who's that?"

Captain Meaker shouted, "The fire department! You got some troubles?"

The voice called back, "You ain't got no PO-lice with you? If you got th' PO-lice, I ain't lettin' you in here!"

The captain glanced toward Luis and me and shook his head. "No, there's no PO-lice out here. You gonna let us in or shall we go back home?"

I noticed with amusement how the captain pronounced "PO-lice." He usually spoke with a cultured voice that carried a hint of New England. In fact, his lack of what I called "jungle jive" had surprised me at first. I'd noticed, too, that he'd lapse into jungle jive from time to time when he was talking to other Blacks. It usually just seemed funny. But this time, in the mood I was in that morning, I thought darkly: Yeah. He's reverting to his true ways. Real ape man stuff!

The door opened a slight crack. A tall brown man peered out. He looked past us—checking for the PO-lice, I figured. Then he opened the door and stepped aside. Luis and I followed the captain. The room's atmosphere was stifling with cigarette smoke and other odors too numerous to identify. Empty beer and wine bottles littered both furniture and floor. Looking into the kitchen I could see a sink and table stacked with dirty dishes and leftover food. One corner of the kitchen was piled full of garbage—bagged and unbagged.

A baby cried in another room. I saw, and smelled, used disposable diapers scattered among the litter that filled the place. On the other side of the living room a little girl sat watching cartoons, seeming oblivious to what was happening behind her.

The man led us into a bedroom where a young woman sprawled naked across the bed, her legs dangling into the space between the bed and a crib full of piled clothing where the crying baby also lay. I felt a familiar disgust. Disgust for the people who seemed to choose, so easily, to live lives full of alcohol and drugs and who knew what else. The South Valley was full of them.

I laughed inwardly at the naked girl sprawled on the bed and thought, grimly, that she'd just got what she had coming. But from where I was standing I could look in both directions and see the little girl in the living room still motionless in front of cartoons and the baby kicking and crying in its filthy crib.

Something vague began gnawing at my stomach as I watched the children. Luis and the captain bent over the bed and looked at the woman. Luis held his fingertips against her throat while Captain Meaker flipped her eyelids open to look into her dilated pupils. Luis lifted one of her arms and felt the muscles around her neck and shoulder. He said quietly, "Stiff. Looks like about six hours or so."

The captain nodded. Then he turned to the tall man. "She's dead," he said with no emotion. "Been dead most of the night. You her husband?"

"Me? Hey, man, I ain't nothin'. I was jist here fer awhile las' night and when I woke up this mornin' I come in here an' that's how she was. Man, I didn't have nothin' t' do with none o' this!"

The captain nodded. "Booter," he said, turning toward me, "why don't you pick up the baby, get the little girl and take them out to the Engine. Tell Don to call the police and ask them to come in quiet. I think we have an overdose here."

I looked at the girl on the bed—she hadn't really become a woman yet—as I moved toward the crib. I could see needle tracks up and down the arm that lay pointed toward me. I could see tracks on the insides of both her wasted thighs, down the shins of her legs, even across the tops of her feet. The search for open veins for her needles had taken this girl to some mighty interesting places. I picked up the baby. Its diaper squished all over me.

WHEN THE BRAVE ONES CRIED

As I headed for the living room I could hear the tall brown man objecting loudly, "Hey, man. Give me a little break. Can't you wait 'til I gets clear o' here afore you calls the PO-lice? I called you 'cause I think maybe you can help her. I didn't *have* t'call ya. But I didn't wanta leave them kids here alone with that stiff. Y'know what I mean? C'mon, man, I'm fried if the cops finds me here. . . ."

The man's voice was taking an angry edge, and I noticed that Captain Meaker was standing sideways, legs apart, hands ready in a defensive stance. His face still wore its usually pleasant expression, but his powerful body was tense—ready for any move the other man might make.

Luis whispered to me, "Make it quick. These things can get nasty!"

I carried the crying baby and collected the mute, unresisting little girl from in front of the television set. As I stepped out the door into fresher air, I was relieved to see two policemen coming down the hall. They must have been on another call, but when I said, "Hey, F. D. needs some help in there," they nodded and quickly slipped into the apartment.

"Whatta ya got?" Don asked as I approached the Engine.

Using the radio code for reporting a death, I said, "A nine-oh-one. Looks like an overdose."

Don nodded and reached for the baby. He opened a rear compartment door and pulled out one of the large trauma dressings we keep in our supplemental first aid kit. Laying the baby on the running board beside his pump controls, Don changed its diaper with the calm assurance of an experienced father. Then he stood and held the infant against his barrel chest. He tried to sooth it with his rich baritone voice but the baby kept screaming. Don looked into its face. "Hungry?" he asked. "Then wait just a minute."

He handed the baby to me and opened a compartment door. He pulled an irrigating syringe from a first aid kit and filled it with Gatorade from a jug in another compartment. He took the baby from me and stuck the end of the syringe in the baby's mouth. There was immediate quiet. He eased himself down to sit on the running board beside the pump panel.

Don examined the baby's arms and legs. They were as thin as pencils. "Was it his mother who checked out?"

I shrugged. "I don't know—probably."

"What was she on? Heroin?"

I nodded.

"Thought so. Look how thin this little one is. He's either malnourished or addicted or both."

"Addicted?"

Don nodded. "Sure. Babies of addicts are generally addicted themselves at birth."

I sat down on the running board near him. The idea of a baby heroin addict sent a lump deep into the pit of my stomach. Suddenly the little girl, still mute, crawled up beside me and sat as close as she could. I'm not sure why I did it, but I put my arm around her. She snuggled even closer and then climbed onto my lap where she immediately went to sleep.

We sat like that for a long time until one of the police officers took her and placed her in the back seat of his patrol car.

. . . .

We ran to a couple of automobile accidents and to help a woman who had slipped on a wet floor in a store. Supper that evening was quick. It was Friday again and we avoided a big meal on Friday nights. The tones usually didn't give us time for that luxury.

Sure enough, I had just opened my bottle of pop when the tones erupted from the ceiling. "Engine Five. An EMS assignment. 2620 South Dyer, Apartment 1415. 2620 South Dyer, Apartment 1415. Reported stabbing. Exercise caution. Police are running with you."

A police car, running hot with siren and lights screaming, turned in front of us at the intersection of 26th and Dyer. We followed it into the maze around the highrise ghetto. Two other police cars were already there. We followed the officers into the building and into the elevator. Creaking, the elevator lifted us to the fourteenth floor. The policemen drew their revolvers, holding them inconspicuously by their sides, fingers carefully off the triggers, as we followed them out and down the hall.

Loud shouts in English and Spanish echoed. We turned a corner. I could see two policemen wrestling with a short, stubby Mexican who was shouting curses as he fought. They pinned him to the floor.

A cop wearing sergeant's stripes clipped handcuffs on him and jerked him to his feet.

Inside, a young woman in a police uniform was holding three more men at bay with a shotgun while they cursed and yelled at her. Another man, his face pale, sat in a chair beside the kitchen sink, holding a bloody towel against his lower abdomen. Captain Meaker and Luis slid the wounded man to the floor while I pulled the blood pressure cuff from the bag I carried. I checked his pressure while the captain and Luis peeked under the towel.

I heard the captain grunt. "What did he use on you?" he asked.

The man shook his head silently. Luis spoke to him in Spanish. The man replied in a weak voice. "A straight razor," Luis said to the captain.

The captain nodded. "I thought so. It's a straight, clean cut." I was writing down pulse and blood pressure information as the captain lifted the towel again. He said, "Hey, Booter, here's a good one to learn on. Let Luis handle that end and you come take care of this guy. He's got some intestine hanging out."

The police were scuffling with another of the men behind us as I lifted the towel and looked under it. It hadn't taken long for me to develop a pretty strong stomach, so I looked at the anatomy bulging in front of me with a sort of clinical detachment. I pulled plastic wrap from the kit, wet the protruding intestine with sterile saline solution, covered it with sterile plastic and placed a loose bandage over it. The ambulance crew arrived just as we finished.

The police were leading the group of handcuffed men out of the building as we walked back to Engine 5. I was hungry. We got back to the station and warmed our supper. We almost finished before the tones called again.

. . . .

"Engine Five. An EMS call. 1842 South 25th. 1842 South 25th. Reported stabbing with two victims. Use caution. The police are running with you."

Luis stuffed another bite into his mouth and Don remarked dryly, "I wish sometimes that I had the concession for knives and guns down here." We were out the door in less than thirty seconds.

Don wheeled the Engine up in front of the house just as the second police car pulled up. We bailed out, grabbed our kits, and headed for the front door of a dirty little house that once had been painted an awful shade of pink. A police woman opened the front door and motioned us inside. She led us to the kitchen where a young man sat in an old chair. His hands were handcuffed behind his back. A large stain of blood spread down his bare chest and across his pants. I was surprised when I noticed he was white.

Another man lay sprawled on the floor near the back door. Two police officers crouched beside him. One of them was holding pressure on a towel that surrounded a large knife that stuck out of the prone man right where his belly button should have been. I clapped the sphygmomanometer onto his arm and pumped the cuff while the captain felt for a pulse. The man groaned and tried to move.

Captain Meaker spoke into his radio, requesting a paramedic unit. The dispatcher told him none was available. He made a noise like a flattening tire. That was when I noticed the boy. He stood just behind me and stared, wide-eyed, at the scene. He was about ten years old, dressed only in ragged cut-offs and several days' dirt.

Luis was beside the handcuffed man who cursed and kicked at him as he tried to examine the wound in his chest. Luis shrugged his shoulders and backed off. "Luis," Captain Meaker called. "This one's bleeding out internally. Get the MAST trousers ready."

I tried the blood pressure again. "I get eighty-five over thirty," I told the captain. Then I added with a tone of doubt, "That can't be right, can it?"

"Probably," the captain replied grimly. "I'd guess that blade got his liver. He's going out fast."

There wasn't much bleeding around the wound. I had trouble imagining how the guy could be bleeding out with no sign of more blood. But Captain Meaker guided my hand to the man's abdomen. "See how distended it is here?" he asked. "Palpate it—thump on it—right here."

I did. It felt like a water balloon under my fingers. Even so, I objected. "Yeah, but the knife's too low. It should've missed his liver."

"No, see how it's angled upward. Judging from the size of the handle I'd say he has about ten inches of steel stuck in him. It got his liver all right—and a few other things too, most likely."

Luis had the MAST trousers spread out. We carefully rolled the man and slipped the rubber pants under him. I fastened the legs while the captain carefully closed it as best he could around the protruding knife. Luis began pumping the suit up, starting with the legs first.

I thought, those MAST trousers are the handiest things to come out of a factory in a long time. I knew they'd been developed by the military for battlefield wounds. You slip them onto a person and pump them up so they exert pressure evenly all around the victim's legs and lower body. The pressure forces blood back into circulation to relieve shock. In cases of internal bleeding they act like a full-body pressure bandage to slow the loss of blood.

"Get the pressure again," Captain Meaker ordered me.

I pumped the cuff. "A little better. Ninety-five over fifty."

An ambulance crew pulled a stretcher into the room just as we finished. We helped load, and I noticed with some amusement how a younger man who seemed to be observing the work of the two ambulance attendants kept staring, wide-eyed, at the knife handle. One of the attendants noticed and whispered with a smile, "He's doing observation for his EMT class."

I couldn't help it. I just had to let some of my superiority show. I nodded gravely at the trainee while they were closing the ambulance doors. "Gets kind of rough down here sometimes. But don't worry, you'll get used to it soon enough."

He nodded, but I could see him trying to make up his mind about his future in the business.

. . . .

Don started the Engine. I head Captain Meaker say, "Dispatch. Engine Five's available."

Immediately, the dispatcher replied, "Ten-four, Engine Five is available and a call. Engine Five, stand by. . . ."

Don idled by the curb waiting for the address. I watched the police loading the other wounded man into a police car, a small bandage covering part of his chest. The boy stood alone, close by, watching the whole thing. He seemed so small, alone, and bewildered that I was ready to get down to see if I could do anything for him when the dispatcher's voice came again. "Engine Five. An EMS assignment. Woman injured in a fall. 2840 South 28th. 2840 South 28th. Woman injured in a fall."

I watched the boy as long as I could see him. I wondered where he fit into the little drama I had just seen. A vague feeling of anger rose inside me as I wondered what *his* future would hold.

It was a short run to 2840 South 28th. We pulled to a stop in front of a small, neatly painted white house with black trim. The lawn was still green and a few fall flowers decorated the garden; it was a marked contrast to the squalor around it. We were hurrying across the lawn when the door opened, and a big Black man stepped out. He wore a clergyman's collar.

"You were very quick. Thank you," were his first words. Then, as he led us inside, "I check on her every day. I called this evening, but she wouldn't answer the phone, so I came over to see what was wrong and found her like this."

A frail looking elderly Black lady lay on the floor. She was obviously in pain. Captain Meaker knelt beside her. "What happened, M'am?" he asked gently.

"I jist come from th' grocery an' I foun' two boys in here. Right here inside my house! I guess I scared 'em, 'cause they run out right past me. I tried t' grab fer one of 'em, but he knocked me down an' I guess I broke something in my shoulder. I couldn't get up."

The captain nodded. Gently he began to probe her shoulder while I started getting vital signs. Luis spoke into the captain's radio, calling for an ambulance.

Her vitals were good, and I listened while the captain carefully splinted the broken shoulder. "Thank goo'ness fer Rev'rend Thomas here," the woman said. "I dunno how long I'd 'a layed here if t'want fer him."

The minister knelt beside the captain holding the woman's hand in his. I watched, impressed by the tenderness of the big Black man and by the way Captain Meaker was treating her. It struck me then that no matter who the captain was dealing with, he treated all of them with the same courteous respect. We had joked and hardened ourselves while we'd been taking our Emergency Medical Technician training at the Academy. And, with many of the men on the Department, joking and callousness had carried over onto the job.

They treated the dirtier and poorer patients with a sort of tolerance—but not respect.

A police officer came into the room. He asked the woman questions about what had been an apparent burglary. "I don' know what they be wantin'," she said. "I ain't got much fer anybody t' take. An' they was jist *little* boys, too. Why, they couldn't a'been more'n about ten or eleven. . . ."

The policeman muttered, rather noncommittally, "Don't worry, we'll find 'em."

"Well," said the lady gently, "don't be too hard on 'em if you do. They prob'ly jist like all th' other kids down here. Most likely don' even know who their mommas and pappas are. . . ."

I looked around the house. It was as neat inside as it was outside. I couldn't help contrasting it with the apartment we'd been in that morning. Pictures of three or four children hung on the wall. What, I wondered, was a woman like this doing in a neighborhood like this? Why didn't she move to someplace where she could be safe?

I looked down at her brown face, creased with age and pain. She was staring straight at me. She smiled. "You look like you're jist 'bout th' same age as my youngest boy. He's in Germany with th' army." Her face contorted momentarily with pain before she asked, "Could I ask you t' get me a drink o' water? I'm so mighty thirsty."

I hurried to the kitchen sink, found a clean glass in one of the cabinets, filled it with cold water and returned to her. I felt a sudden rising of hot anger as I gently lifted her head and held the glass to her lips. She drank while I thought darkly of how a woman like this could become a victim in her own home.

"Thank you," she smiled when she had finished. "Y'know, I don't think you has any idea how much some o' us people down here appreciates what you all does t' pertect us. I knows yer work is dangerous, an' ever' time I sees yer fire truck goin' down th' road, I prays fer you. Yer mother must be mighty proud o' you—helpin' other people like me ever' day. An' it don't even matter to you that I'm black as a coal lump an' yer white. Things has sure changed, though. I kin 'member a time when there jist weren't no help anywhere fer a old black woman down here. . . ."

We helped the ambulance crew—the same ones who'd run on our first stabbing—carry her out. While we carried her, I asked a question I'd been nursing for a long time. "Why do you stay here? Why don't you move to a better part of town?"

She squeezed my hand. "Son; some o' us ain't as lucky as you. Our skin weren't th' same color as yours an' when th' time come fer us t' make our choices, we di'n't have as many to choose from. Now, my choices are gone. I *can't* leave here."

The ambulance crew set the front wheels of the stretcher on the back lip of the ambulance and slid it in. One of them was just closing the door when I gave in to a sudden impulse and scrambled in beside the gurney. I took her hand in mine and said with more emotion than I'd allowed myself in a long, long time, "M'am. . .M'am, here's my card. If I can *ever* help you in any way, you just call me! And I mean that! I really do!" I handed her one of the little business cards the Department makes us carry and crawled out of the ambulance.

Captain Meaker stood by the door, watching me. I felt absolutely foolish over what I'd just done, so I tried to excuse myself by saying, "Little old ladies get to me. I guess they remind me of my grandmother, or something."

I kept waiting for someone to make some kind of funny comment. No one did, but the captain caught my sleeve between his fingers. He whispered, "I think you might be starting to learn, Booter. You just might be. . . ."

The Reverend, the captain, Luis and I stood on the sidewalk watching the ambulance drive away. Then the Reverend Thomas stretched his hand toward Captain Meaker. "I'm Reverend Daniel Thomas."

"Dave Meaker."

The minister nodded his head and smiled broadly. "So you're Dave Meaker? I've been hearing about you ever since I moved to the Valley. Been intending to get over to meet you for a long time—but you know how time slips away. I've heard so much about you; now it's a real pleasure to meet you."

The captain was just starting to answer when Don interrupted. "Are we available? The dumpster in the park is going again."

We rolled to the park and doused the dumpster for the fourth time that week. A couple more EMS calls kept us out until after one in the morning. But when I got back to the station and tried to sleep, I found I was so wide awake, I just lay rigid in bed.

. . . .

It seemed hot in the bunk room. I finally got up and slipped into the kitchen. There I plunked some coins into the pop machine and opened the bottle while I stepped onto the front porch. I closed the door and settled into the porch swing that hung by chains from the overhead.

I sat in the darkness. The city's incessant sounds were quieter at that time of the morning—just a dull throbbing that seemed to come from everywhere at once. It was chilly. I pulled my service jacket tighter around my neck. A gentle breeze rustled dry morning-glory vines that clung to the trellis beside the swing.

My mind kept drifting backward while I sat there. Almost all the runs we'd made from Station 5 since I'd come aboard seemed to run like instant replays. I almost felt the cold wetness of the dead boy in the canal against my chest. I smelled again stale odors of the highrise ghetto, the adult book stores, and bars we'd been called to. I remembered faces of people whose names I had never known and never would know. I remembered the shootings, stabbings, two suicides—the victims—people who, through no fault of their own, happened to be in wrong places at the wrong times.

I remembered voices and snatches of words. I remembered the prostitute beside the canal. I remembered the old woman that evening. I kept hearing her words: "Some o' us jist don't have as many choices as you do." And I remembered the baby that morning—its body addicted from the moment of birth—and I dismissed the idea of choices.

That same anger rose again—a baseless, empty anger I couldn't seem to focus on any one thing or any person. That little girl—sitting on my lap—she could have been my little niece except for circumstances of geography, color, luck and whatever else separated her and her world from me and my world.

I thought of the little boy, David, at the day care center in the old Baptist church. I wondered what kind of place he called home.

I thought of the Reverend Thomas and found myself thinking, "What a fine man!" I couldn't imagine Father Lambert, or any of the other priests at St. Stephanie's, taking enough time and interest in one of their parishioners to check on them personally every day. Too busy with Bingo games, I thought sarcastically.

Then my thoughts turned to Captain Meaker as I remembered the reverend's words beside the little house that night. I heard good things about my captain, too. I gathered that, in the South Valley at least, David Meaker was some sort of living legend.

I remembered a night early in my days at Station 5 when we'd responded on a man down call. We had found an old white wino lying in a gutter beside a state liquor store. The man had been drowning in his own vomit. I watched, stricken, while the captain cleared the derelict's mouth with his fingers and handkerchief. My stomach churned when he placed his mouth over the wino's and blew into him while we struggled to get a balky bag mask working. I remembered his answer when I'd asked him how he could do such a thing. "Well, Booter," he'd said in his quiet way, "he's one of God's children, too. And sometimes the line we walk is very thin—yep, sometimes the line between a person like him and a person like us is mighty thin."

I think it was the night on the station porch that I began to realize I'd never get around to asking for a transfer. That was when I decided to ask Captain Meeker some questions, the next time I had a chance.

Then, in the communications office, a dispatcher punched a button that sent a radio pulse to our receivers and the house lights came on in Station 5. I could hear the dispatcher's voice from the speakers inside. "Engine Five. Freeway milepost 243, eastbound. Freeway milepost 243, eastbound. A vehicle fire. Use channel three."

I grabbed the doorknob and realized that I'd locked myself out.

Chapter Nine

My days off that week included Saturday and Sunday. I went over to Linda's Saturday morning and helped her prepare for the student teaching assignment she had coming in January. Between that, quarter final exams, and plans for our wedding, her life was filled up just then. I helped cut and paste cute little bears, raccoons, and a bunch of giraffes. Then we addressed about a thousand wedding invitations.

"Captain Meaker?" she asked.

"What about him?"

"What's his address?"

I stopped and thought for a moment. "Maybe we'd better not send an invitation to him. I don't think Dad would take to having a Black man and his wife at the bash."

Linda shook her head. "That's not right. You can't leave him out and invite the others from your station."

"I didn't plan to invite the others. You know my father. Can you imagine what he'd say about a Black and a Mexican? Especially when he knows they're both Mormons?"

Linda gnawed on the end of her pen. "I'm going to invite them anyway. Now, what's Captain Meaker's address?"

"I don't know. He lives up near Mountain Park, but I don't know the street or number."

"Find out," Linda's tone let me know there'd be no arguing.

I shrugged and figured they probably wouldn't come anyway.

. . . .

We went to Mass the next morning with my mother. She insisted it wouldn't be proper for Linda and me to have a church wedding without attending church at least once or twice beforehand. I felt vaguely uncomfortable as I dipped my fingers in the holy water, crossed myself and genuflected before I entered the Sanctuary.

The ornamented interior of the old cathedral was familiar, but strangely uncomfortable. As a boy, I'd spent a lot of hours on those benches. I'd served priests at that altar countless times. But it all seemed so long ago. . . .

Linda and I held hands while we followed through the rituals. The priest's voice rose and fell and echoed between stone walls, back and forth under the great, vaulted ceiling. My mind was wandering again, back to scenes and memories I'd explored on the station's porch. The litany seemed far away. Twice I missed a cue and had to be reminded to kneel or stand.

When it was over and we were filing out the great doors, I looked back—back to the statuary, paintings, and candles glowing by side altars and I felt a familiar emptiness rising inside me.

. . . .

We drove up into one of the canyons that crease the mountains outside our city. Cottonwoods had lost most of their leaves. A chill wind blew between the canyon walls. We left the car at a turnout to walk hand in hand up a small path that seemed to lead nowhere in particular.

We walked for a long time in silence before I ventured, "It's just not the same somehow. . . ."

"What's not the same?"

"Church."

Linda squeezed my hand. "How do you mean?"

"I don't know." I shook my head to sort my thoughts into something she could understand—something *I* could understand.

We came to a small stream that wandered between shallow banks, tripping over stones and pebbles. Beside a tiny waterfall we sat in silence while I tossed bits of wood and rock into the water.

"I don't know. . . ," I said again. I shifted around to look at her. "This morning, listening to the priest, it hit me that it's always the same. Y'know what I mean?"

She shook her head.

"I mean, it's always—well, heck, it's always the *same!* There's never any *feeling* in it. It's always just. . . *words!* It's like a ritual we listen to but don't ever feel for." Again I added, "D'you know what I mean?"

This time Linda nodded. "Yes," she sighed. "Yes, I know exactly what you mean. I've been feeling that way, too, for a couple of years now. I don't quite understand it myself. All I know is that something is missing—but I don't know exactly what."

That surprised me. I told her so. "But, Linda. . . you go to church almost every week. . . ."

"Yes," she sighed again. "I go and I go through the motions, but my heart isn't with me."

I nodded. We sat for a long time in silence before she spoke again, "I've been going to the same church all my life, but I think my family and I could drop off the end of the earth and no one would notice. And, like you said, it's all words—the same words, week after week. I can't seem to feel hope any more—yet I keep going, week after week, hoping it will change somehow. . . but it never does."

We sat close together until the sun slipped behind the mountain, and we grew cold in the shade.

. . . .

Monday was cold and clear. The first real winter winds were blowing down the valley as Thanksgiving approached. We were called to a first alarm at General Hospital and staged a couple of blocks away while some other companies, a Bat Chief, and a Division Chief went in to investigate what was apparently a false alarm.

Captain Meaker, Don, Luis and I were huddled together by the Engine's exhaust pipe, trying to keep warm, when the captain spoke.

"Oh, hey, Booter," he said. "This is Monday. We usually have a family evening on Monday when we're home. We decided to have one at the station this evening. I tried to call you yesterday but your mother said you were out romancing. Would you like to invite your parents and Linda to come down? We'll have supper then sing songs and play games with the kids."

I nodded and surprised myself. But it seemed like a good idea. My father was away on the truck and both Linda and my mother had been wanting to visit the station. "Okay," I said. "I'll call them when we get back."

The hospital alarm turned out to be a faulty sensor in the alarm system. We spent the rest of the day inspecting stores and apartment houses. The apartment houses scared me. Most of them were old, crowded with people, and built of wood with brick veneer. Open stairways had no fire doors. Fire escapes were rusty and shaky. "Deathtraps," I muttered.

"What?" asked Don.

"Deathtraps," I repeated. "These places are deathtraps! Why doesn't someone do something about tightening up fire code enforcement in these places?"

Don shrugged. "We try every year," he answered dryly. "The Union's lobbyists go up to Capitol Hill and yell and fuss, but no one ever listens. We can't even get smoke alarms put into these traps."

"But why?"

Don laughed a short, cold laugh. "I'll give you three guesses and the first two won't count." He paused. "It's money, Boot! Just plain, cold, green money. Who owns all these places? Sure as heck it's not the people who live in them! We've been trying for years to get fire doors, smoke and central alarms, repair on fire escapes, and a few other things. But people who own these slums have a lot of clout up on the Hill and in city council. Hecksfire, half the turkeys in those offices own places like these themselves!"

Don was warming up to his subject. "And who gives a diddle about people down here? So a place burns and takes a few of them with it? Big deal! It makes good pictures—firemen carrying out dead bodies—and good pictures sell newspapers. There's a big flurry of righteous concern. Politicians make loud and lofty promises they know they won't have to keep because everyone will forget all about it a week later. . . ."

"No, Boot, it's just good business and good politics to let one of these places go up once in a while. Why, the owners can even write the loss off their income taxes!"

"But what about *us?* We have to fight the fires in these dumps. Can't we get them to enforce laws for the sake of firefighters?"

Don didn't answer. Instead he gave me a look that let me know the answer—a look that said "stupid question." I thought wryly that if a picture of a fireman carrying a dead child from a tenement is good copy for newspapers, what must pictures of dead firemen be?

. . . .

I called Mom and Linda at lunch time. Both were enthusiastic about visiting the station.

We got back to the stationhouse a little late and found Don's family already there. His wife was bustling around the kitchen and their two kids were sprawled in front of the television. Don introduced May, his wife, and tried to introduce Emma and Kimball, but they were too engrossed in an afternoon re-run to be very sociable.

A few minutes later Luis escorted his wife in. She was a tiny but very pretty woman with delicate brown features—the kind of woman you picture when you think of a classic Spanish dancer. She carried a small bundle in her arms, and we all gathered around and clucked our appreciation of little Juanito with his big, amazed black eyes.

Linda drove up with my mother, and I made introductions. Then I proudly took them on the grand tour. We were just leaving the bunk room when the back door burst open and six kids spilled into the hallway.

We followed their pell-mell progress into the dayroom and found Captain Meaker tossing the smallest two into the air. A moment later he introduced us to his wife, Ellen, and a rainbow of children. I saw immediately that one of them was white, one was Chinese or Japanese, and four were various shades of black. The white child was obviously retarded.

He introduced the black ones first. "This is David, Junior," he said as a shy boy of about twelve stepped forward and offered his hand. "And this is Carla, she's ten. Over here is Angie, she's just nine. And these three are our current crop of foster children; Kenneth, who is Japanese, Bryan and Richie."

Kenneth was about ten or so. Richie, whose brown skin and mixed features spoke of uncertain parentage, was about four or five. Bryan, whose eyes and face betrayed his mental handicap, was about the same age. They all stepped forward to shake my hand. Bryan immediately began trying to crawl up my leg.

We dragged the ping-pong table in from the bunk room, added a couple of folding chairs the women had brought with them and soon had enough room for all of us to sit together for supper. We pulled the volleyball net across the apparatus bay and soon had a rollicking game going. Even Kimball Spencer left the television set and joined us.

We played hard until the women called us for supper. Don asked a blessing on the food and I suddenly realized I felt no discomfort about it. I still felt a little uneasy when we knelt together each morning, but the blessing at dinner left me feeling good inside.

Bryan, for some reason only he understood, had taken a liking to me. He insisted on sitting *between* Linda and me at the table. Captain Meaker tried to convince him that we should be allowed to sit together, but Linda and I both assured him we could survive apart for a few minutes. Linda helped the boy with his food. While we ate, we talked. Soon it seemed we'd known all of them for years instead of minutes. I was glad I'd called my mother and Linda—and glad they'd been able to come.

We ate and cleaned up the dishes. Don was just gathering everyone together in the dayroom for songs and games when he was interrupted by a loud banging at the front door. I opened it and found an elderly Black man standing there. He was excited and had trouble getting his messege out. "Firemen," he finally managed to gasp, "y'know thet church over on 22nd by Dyer? Thet Cathedral o' th' MAG-do-LINE? Well, sir, there's an awful lot o' smoke a'comin' out o' it!"

"Cap!" I hollered. "Man here says there's smoke coming from the Cathedral of the Magdeline!"

Captain Meeker nodded quickly. He grabbed the microphone of the station's radio while the rest of us headed for the engine bay. I could see that the kids all knew what to do. They stood back to let us pass then the whole crowd followed us out to where our big Engine stood waiting. I stepped into my boots, pulled up the bunker pants and was fastening them when I saw Linda standing by the door watching me. She wasn't smiling like the kids were.

I grabbed the rail and was starting to pull myself into my seat when my mother grabbed my arm and held it. She pecked an embarrassing kiss on my cheek and said, "Oh, please, be careful!"

The captain was swinging into his seat beside Don as I pulled my helmet into place and began fastening the front of my coat. Don hit the starter. The big Cummins roared to life beside me. We began to roll carefully out the door while all over the bay the smaller children jumped up and down with excitement. I caught a glimpse of Linda. She was holding Bryan in her arms, and my mother, beside her, was wiping tears from her eyes.

We swung left into traffic. Don shoved the accelerator all the way down while the captain ran the electronic siren with one hand and the microphone with the other. We hit the first intersection just as I heard the dispatcher put the call out to the other stations.

"First alarm assignment," she said in her monotonous, calm voice. "Engine Five, Engine Twenty-two, Engine Six, Engine Fourteen. Ladder Twenty-two, Ladder Six, Ladder Twelve. Battalion Seven. Utility One. First alarm at the Cathedral of the Magdeline. Cathedral of the Magdeline, Dyer and 22nd. Dyer and 22nd. Citizen reports smoke from the church."

I watched cars we passed. I still had that little feeling inside that set me apart from the people who watched as we rolled past. I heard our siren and blaster echoing back to us from the storefronts. I could see our reflection flashing back at us from windows. Don dodged a semi-truck at one intersection, and, for a second, I thought we were going to roll over. Through it all I kept seeing Linda and my mother as we had moved out the door. I kept seeing the looks on their faces.

And I remembered the looks on the faces of the other women waiting back there. They were all the same. I knew my thought was a little melodramatic, but I realized they were all women who watched men they loved head off into battle in the most dangerous job in America today.

But I didn't have time to dwell on that. I turned and craned my neck. I could see the cathedral's tower ahead, above the roofs of other buildings. As we approached, I thought I could see a thin vapor of gray spreading across the street. I heard the captain's voice in the radio speaker. "Dispatch, Engine Five. Smoke showing at the cathedral. Engine Five will take the hydrant at Dyer and 22nd and enter for search. Engine Twenty-two come in behind Engine Five and back us up inside. Other units stage. Engine Five is passing command to Battalion Three. . .Ah, correction. . .I mean Battalion Seven."

We paused beside the hydrant. As I dropped off, wrench in hand, I heard Captain Meaker's voice again. "Dispatch, Engine Five. This smoke is extensive. It's coming from the eaves all around the building. Give us a second alarm on this one."

I glanced toward the building as I pulled hose from the bed. Smoke was rolling from under the roof line all around and smoke was beginning to puff from the top of the spire. I looked up and saw the captain standing in his open cab door. "Boot!" he hollered. "Lay a set of doubles!"

I pulled a second hose from the back and dragged both of them toward the hydrant. I was opening the caps when Engine Five began rolling toward the church laying its hoses behind.

Chapter 10

Luis and the captain already had a two-and-a-half-inch hose pulled up the stairs and through the big front doors of the church by the time I caught up to Engine 5. Don signalled that he had a good water supply, so I pulled on my SCBA and followed the hose into the church's mammoth interior. I could hear Luis and Captain Meaker scuffing along somewhere inside, so I dropped to my knees, gripped the hose, and started crawling along it toward them. The smoke was so thick you couldn't see your hand in front of your face, but there wasn't much heat.

I caught up with them about halfway down the main aisle. We paused to hold a conference. "This is a bit scary," the captain said, using a firefighter's typical understatement. "There must be an awfully hot fire somewhere in here to have filled a building this big with this much smoke. I've got a feeling it's in a closed space and has damped down. If it gets air all of a sudden, things could become mighty interesting in here."

I knew well enough that when a firefighter says a situation was "interesting" he means he was scared out of his wits. That made me nervous. If the captain thought things could get interesting, I wasn't sure I wanted to be there.

"Let's get this place searched out fast. We'll take the right side. Stay close." Then, into his radio, "Engine Twenty-two, Engine Five. We're searching the east side of the main floor. Can you take the west?" We left the heavy hose lying in the middle aisle and split up. Even though there was little chance that anyone was in the building, we still had to look. I scrambled along the right side of the pews checking small side altar spaces that lined the cathedral on both sides in alcoves under the huge, stained-glass windows. Votive candles created eerie little patches of glow in the thick smoke. I'd been in this church several times when I was younger, and even though I hardly thought of myself as a good Catholic any more, it hurt to think that such a beautiful place might soon be in ruins.

I slid down the side, shining my flashlight down each pew space as I went. The place was in thermal balance, with stratifications of smoke grading down from the invisible vaulted ceiling high overhead. Down low the air was clear. By ducking under the smoke I could see anything lying on the floor.

I reached the back of the church, crossed behind the pews, and ran in a low crouch back up the center aisle toward the altar where the captain was still groping around. I joined him there, followed in a moment by Luis.

"I never knew there were was this much stuff scattered around up here," the captain said through his mask's speaker port. We crawled together behind the main altar toward the console of the cathedral's huge pipe organ.

"Whoa!" called Captain Meaker. He pulled one of his gloves off and felt the floor. I did the same. It was blistering hot. "I think we just found the fire," he said.

The captain pulled his portable radio from its pocket. "Battalion Seven, Engine Five. We're up around the altar and have found a hot floor. I think we have a basement fire in the building's north end."

The radio speaker crackled as the Bat and Division Chiefs relayed our news and redeployed their forces. I noticed curls of smoke wisping up between the floor boards and I could feel heat penetrating my heavy pants where I knelt. I never have felt comfortable knowing I was crawling around on a thin floor above a fire, and I sure didn't feel comfortable then. I don't know if it was just my imagination, but I thought I could hear a dull rumble like a fire rolling under me.

The captain shouted, "Let's finish checking this place and get out of here."

I was all for that. I crawled toward the choir loft on the right side of the altar and began checking for victims. I hadn't been up there long when the alarm bell on my SCBA began to ring—a signal that

I had five minutes of air left. The captain's bell began to ring on the other side of the sacristy. I had only one more row to check.

I finished and started to scramble down the steps when my air pack's harness caught on something. Just then I heard another sound that almost congealed my blood—a sound that started as a long, low screech. Lumber grinding against itself. I looked upward thinking the roof was coming in on us.

I heard Captain Meaker. "Out! Out! Get out!" I heard his bell and Luis's bell retreating toward the back of the church. The grinding of the collapse grew louder. I pulled and tugged at my trapped harness, but it wouldn't give. The bell kept up its jangled warning. As I tugged and fought I needed more and more air. Air was coming harder now. I had to fight for each breath.

I began to yell as loud as I could, but I knew that my voice, muffled by my mask, was being drowned out by racket of the grinding, collapsing roof.

I was fighting back panic, trying to pull myself together to think. I'd run out of air many times in training. Instructors had seen to that to give me a feel for it and to teach me emergency procedures. I knew I could unfasten my mask's hose and tuck it inside my coat for a little protection from smoke and heat, but I knew, too, that it was a long way back to the door outside.

The grinding grew. Now I could hear things begin to fall. I crouched between the rows of choir chairs, hoping they'd shelter me some when the roof came all the way down. Then, with a sudden crash and a huge puff of rolling flame, the organ console and the entire Great Altar fell into the basement. Flames rolled out of the basement and licked up the sacristy wall. A bright light filled the entire church, flickering back and forth, rolling with thick, boiling smoke.

The roar of flames finished the job. The panic that had begun to rise took hold of me. I jerked against the restraining harness, unbuckling it to break free. If I'd stopped to think, I might have moved backward and freed myself, but now I was getting ready to throw away the only thing that stood between me and certain, smoky death.

Just as my harness opened, I heard a bell ringing right beside me and felt someone pulling on my air tank. I moved backward. Immediately the tank come free of whatever had been holding it. I saw a captain's red helmet beside my face, felt a hand groping around under me, feeling for my air regulator. He found it and checked the pressure/demand switch. I'd already done that and had switched it to the demand setting to save precious air. I just didn't have any air left.

"Booter," a familiar voice called, "follow me out. Do you need to buddy breathe?"

I signaled thumbs up, I was still getting a little air. "Follow me," he called again. "Skip breathe if you have to to save air!"

We crawled out, skirting the blaze that rolled out of the floor while I took a breath, held it as long as I could, exhaled and pulled in another.

We made it to the front door in what must have been record time, fighting our way past several crews who were dragging hoses in to fight the fire from above it.

. . . .

I guess it's a good thing I didn't have time to think, or I might have had trouble going back in. But no sooner had we hit the main door than a Bat Chief grabbed us. "You ready to go back in?"

"Change bottles!" gasped the captain.

"When you get them changed, go in and take a hose down the stairs on the south side. We're holding the fire in one basement room. Pull the ceiling down in the hall to see if the fire's extended from that room."

I knelt on the sidewalk and breathed oxygen while several hands changed my air bottle. I grabbed a cup of Gatorade just as a hand thumped my helmet to tell me I was ready to go again. Luis met us at the door. We followed a hose along the back of the church, down some stairs and into a basement hallway. On the hall floor the nozzle lay untended. Its crew had probably run out of air and retreated.

We picked it up and advanced up the hall to a closed door. I could hear fire on the other side, could hear water pounding in there. In fact, a trickle of water ran under the door. Luis pulled the ceiling with a short pikepole and we checked the dead space for heat and smoke. There was none so we crouched there, waiting and watching.

I heard scuffling in the hall behind me and turned to find the Battalion 4 Chief scrambling toward us. "All clear down here?"

We all gave him thumbs up.

The chief spoke into his radio and then to Captain Meaker. The captain turned toward me. "We get to do it!" he hollered through his mask. "Bust the door, Booter!"

I pulled the Halligan tool from my belt and forced it into the door's lock. One twist and the door sprang open. Luis opened the nozzle as it did and beat the roll of flame that tried to emerge back into the room. We followed retreating flames. Within a few seconds it was dark in there.

We pulled ceiling in two rooms adjacent to the burned room and found no fire. Luis's bell began to ring again. The Bat Chief called for a relief crew. We pulled out as soon as they got there. In a few minutes we were sitting together on Engine 5's tailboard.

"That's the way to do it," said Don, laughing. "Get all the glory for snuffing the fire then pull out so some other company has to overhaul. Luis, you got that bell of yours trained to go off when you want it to?"

"It's all in controlling the breathing," Luis laughed. But a moment later, when the captain had moved away, Luis changed the tone of his voice as he spoke to me. "Booter," he said, "I hope you know what our 'nigger' captain did for you tonight. You'd have broiled in there if he hadn't gone back for you."

I thought about that all the time I was repacking hose.

I knew he was right.

Chapter Eleven

Thanksgiving drew closer and my vague feeling of discontent grew.

I was attending church with Mom and Linda every Sunday that I didn't have duty. Dad went, too, any time he was home with the truck. But the more times I attended Mass the more my feelings of emptiness grew. I tried to talk about those feelings with my father one day.

The Sunday before Thanksgiving was cold and snowy. We returned home from church and Dad and I sat in front of the television football games while Mom and Linda clattered around in the kitchen. I watched the screen absently, my thoughts a thousand miles from the Astroturf world of pro ball. I guess it might have been my timing. . . Dad was caught up in the game when I ventured, "Dad, can I talk with you?"

He grunted, eyes glued to an interception.

"Dad, have you ever felt. . . well, have you ever felt. . . felt dissatisfied?"

"With what?"

"I dunno. Life in general. The Catholic church. . . ."

He smiled, still watching the next play, listening half to the announcer and half to me. "With life—sure. With the church—never. How come you're asking?"

"Because I'm dissatisfied."

"With what?"

"With the church. With life. With the way things are."

He looked at me, and a scowl crossed his face. "Well, that just about covers everything, don't it? What's this nonsense all about, anyway?"

I shook my head. "I don't really know. But things just don't seem right any more. I mean, I'm working with people I always disliked—Blacks, Mexicans, addicts, winos, whores, bums—you name it, I work with it. I even work with some of them at the station—Blacks and Mexicans, I mean. And all of a sudden, I'm starting to think they might not really be so bad."

The announcer was shouting about a touchdown, or something, and my father's mind drifted back to the screen. But I guess that last sentence got his attention. He looked at me and asked in an incredulous tone, "You guess they might not be so *bad?*"

I shook my head again. "No, some of them are really pretty good people. It's more like they just didn't get the breaks like we did. Like we were lucky and they weren't. Like if they had faced different circumstances they might have turned out just like us. Or like if *we* had been in their places. . . . "

A frown crossed Dad's face. "So what's the church have to do with this?"

"I don't know. . .," I sighed, "I just don't know. When I was a kid, the church seemed strong and tough. I believed in it. I even thought once of becoming a priest. But now I just don't seem to have any feelings for it. It's like it's. . . empty. Do you know what I mean? Just empty, and with arguments about politics and people and priests even fighting with the Pope about birth control and stuff like that. . . it's like it's just a place we go every Sunday because that's what we're supposed to do. But it's always the same thing. The priest gets up and gobbles a bunch of meaningless balderdash, and we all sit down and stand up and kneel down and cross ourselves and. . . ."

And I'd gone too far. Dad rose suddenly from his seat on the sofa and stood over me wagging his finger in my face. His face was red as he shouted, "And you . . . you, kid, are too smart for your own good! You think you know more than the priests and the Popes and everyone! Is that it? You know more than your mother and your old man, too! Is that it?"

He paused for air and roared on before I could say anything. "No, that's not it! It's them damn Mormons you've been hanging around! They got their missionaries working on you? They getting you to think like they do? Or maybe it's that nigger and Mex you work with. They getting into your head? Check your skin boy. . . what color is it? Is it still white . . . . or is it turning brown?"

I tried to answer, but he didn't slow down enough to give me a chance. "I'll tell you what, boy. . . I was raised a Catholic and I'll die a Catholic, and I won't *ever* question the church, and if you know what's good for you, you won't question it neither. I wondered why you never got that transfer outta that station. Now I know why. I raised me a damn nigger-lover Mexican. And after I fed you all these years and put up with all your. . . ."

He raised his clenched fist. For a moment I thought he was going to slug me. But he put his fist down, spun around and stomped out through the kitchen, past Mom and Linda, and crashed out the back door. A moment later, he crashed back in, grabbed his jacket and disappeared again.

I sat there, shaking. I looked up to see Mom and Linda, both white-faced, standing in the kitchen door. My mother asked, "What did you *say* to him?"

I shook my head and listened to my father's pickup truck roar backward out of the driveway. Then I got up, pulled on my jacket and left the house, too.

. . . .

I drove aimlessly around the city with a tangle of confused thoughts racing through my mind. I knew Dad would be at a bar someplace. That's where he always heads when things become too much for him. In fact, that didn't seem like such a bad idea at the moment. I drove down to Dudley's and pulled into the parking lot. I started to get out, but then I paused, and finally just sat for a few minutes. Then I turned the key and drove on.

I drifted past the training tower at the Fire Department Academy, on past the airport, into farmland that surrounds the city, back to the South Valley, and past Station 5. I wandered up through the University, the downtown highrises, and out toward Mountain Park.

I drove up the canyon, got out and walked to the little creek which was fringed with ice. I stood for a few moments then, on an impulse I didn't understand, I got back in the truck and drove through the city until I reached St. Stephanie's.

The big front door was locked, so I walked slowly around the building, past the school and its playground, past the convent, and out to the rectory. I rang the bell and waited a long time before the door opened. I asked for Father Lambert. The young lay brother who had answered the door hesitated. "I think he's busy," he said finally.

"I really need to see him," I argued. "He knows me. He was principal of the school when I went here."

The brother with obvious reluctance invited me to step inside. I could smell food cooking and could hear a television set turned to a football game. I waited a long time before I heard someone coming down the hall. It was Father Lambert. In one look I could tell he'd been drinking pretty heavily.

"Confession is in the morning and at six this evening," he said before I'd had a chance to speak.

"I don't want to confess. I just want to talk with you."

Father Lambert scowled. I could smell whiskey on his breath. "You have an appointment?"

I shook my head.

He pulled a little book from his shirt pocket. "How about tomorrow? What time?"

"I have to work tomorrow," I answered and then realized I'd just lied. Tomorrow was another day off.

"The next day, then?"

I shook my head. "I don't know," I replied vacantly, "I'll have to wait and see."

He nodded and said kindly, "Well, my son, you let me know. Do you have our phone number?" I replied that I did, then he asked, "Now, let's see. . . what's your name?"

That surprised me. "You know me," I replied. "I went to St. Stephanie's when you were principal there."

He still shook his head, so I told him my name. I could see it didn't ring any bells. Without saying anything more I turned and left with a heavy, cold feeling of disappointment rising into my chest. I knew that Father Lambert watched me until I turned the corner.

I crawled back into the car and sat for a long time. Then another impulse struck. At the nearest 7-11 store I found a phone booth. I pulled the white pages up on its awkward holder and thumbed through until I found Meaker, David M. . . .

To this day, I don't understand why I did it.

. . . .

His house was on a quiet side street. His truck was parked in front. His car was in the carport. A couple of bicycles were on the front lawn; a basketball lay where it had landed in a flower bed; and in the back yard were a couple of children's swing sets. A tree in the side yard was almost completely filled with a sprawling treehouse made of scraps of lumber and plywood. I drove past the house twice before I stopped and walked slowly to the front door.

The door opened. Little Bryan stood looking up at me. "Is your. . . is your dad home?" I asked, not sure what Bryan might call his foster parent.

The boy disappeared without a word and came back pulling Ellen Meaker by the hand. She was a heavy-set woman who wore the same air of peaceful confidence as her husband. She smiled and came forward, extending her hand. "Come in. Dave's downstairs."

She led me through the kitchen and down the stairs with Bryan following. We went through a family room where the other kids were watching television. She opened a door into a room where there was a workbench, tools, and woodworking equipment. Captain Meaker was working on a finely crafted coffee table. He looked up, saw me, and smiled.

"Well, hello, Booter." He wiped sawdust off his hand and extended it. "What brings you out here on such a miserable day?"

I made a noncommittal reply about the weather and no good games on television. He laughed. "We need days like this now and then, so I can get things done in my workshop." He pulled an old kitchen chair over and motioned for me to sit while he leaned against his workbench.

I ignored the chair he offered and picked up a childish-looking chunk of red two-by-four. Black ladders and hoses were painted on it and "Engine 5" was smeared on the side. He grinned. "Kenneth made that. He's going to be a firefighter when he grows up. Be careful, the paint may not be dry yet."

We made small talk about weather, football, family, the Department, and half a dozen other things before the captain abruptly asked, "Boot, I know you're not here for a social call. You have something you want to talk about. What is it?"

I just shook my head and stood silent for a moment. He waited until I finally spoke. "Well," I began, "I guess I just came by to say 'thank you.' I'd have been fried in that cathedral if you hadn't come back."

He smiled, but shook his head, too. "No, you wouldn't have. You're a good fireman. You'd have worked your way out."

"No," I confessed. "I was starting to panic. I had just unfastened my harness when you found me. I was going to chuck my breathing gear and make a run for it."

"You'd have killed yourself."

"I know. But I was so *scared!*" My voice was trembling. "I've never felt like that before! Never!"

He smiled kindly. "Well, you will again if you stay with this job. You learn to live with it." I guess he could see that what he'd said hadn't made much of a dent, so he added, "Y'know, Boot, that church was an interesting place. I almost wet my pants when that organ started to go through the floor. I thought the roof was coming in on us."

I laughed. "You did? That's what I thought! Man, I've never heard a noise like that!"

We both laughed. "A structural collapse is a noise you don't forget," he agreed.

He stood looking at me while we were silent. Then I asked, "Why did you come back for me?"

"You'd have come back for me, wouldn't you?"

I suddenly realized that I *would* have.

"How'd you find me?" I asked.

"Simple, I just covered my bell with my hand and listened for yours. Crawled right to it."

"Well, thanks. . . ." I said. Then I stood awkwardly drawing little marks with my toe in sawdust that covered the floor.

The captain broke the silence. "What else?"

"What else what?"

"There's something else you came here for."

I nodded. This was becoming difficult. I stammered, "Well,... I wanted to apologize, too."

"For what?"

"For the way I felt at first. About you, I mean."

He was nodding his head as though he already understood and I hadn't even finished talking. "I understand," he said. "But you changed your mind a while ago, didn't you?"

I stared. "You *knew?* You knew how I felt about. . . about working with you?"

"Yes," he nodded as he replied quietly. "When you've been Black as long as I have. . . well, you get to where you can tell."

"And you put up with it?"

"What else could I do? I learned a long time ago that you can't win people unless they want to be won. And the only way to win is with. . . well, with love." He paused, picked up the red fire engine and turned it in his hands. "Remember the poem by Edwin Markham?" he asked. "How's it go? 'Heretic, rebel, a thing to flout. He drew a circle that left me out. But Love and I had wit to win. We drew a circle that took him in.'"

I shook my head, thoroughly ashamed of myself.

"Does it seem strange to talk of love in a firehouse?" he asked almost as though he spoke to himself. "Maybe. But it's hard not to love one another when our lives depend on each other every day. Most people would use the word 'like' instead of 'love.' But it's really the same thing, so why not say so? The strongest love I ever felt was among the Marines in 'Nam when I was a Navy corpsman there. Strongest hatreds, too.

"Someone told me once," he continued, "that you can test your love for someone by imagining how you'd feel if they were suddenly to die."

All of a sudden, I understood.

He stopped talking, and I think both of us were a little embarrassed.

He cleared his throat. "Anyway, Booter, I've seen you changing gradually and it's been a good thing to watch. You're beginning to learn to care, Boot. And caring's what it's all about."

The door opened a crack. Bryan slipped silently into the room. He came directly to me and grabbed my leg until I reached down and picked him up.

"I noticed you with the little girl, that day with the stiff, in the highrise ghetto. I watched you with other kids we've met out there. I watched you and Linda with Bryan the other night at supper. They get to you, don't they? Like him. . . what chance does *he* have with a mind that's not whole? Yet he has an infinite capacity to love and care about others. And what about all those kids out there south of the freeway? What capacity might they have if only someone could help them reach it?"

He paused again and picked up a screwdriver, turned it between his fingers, and put it down again. "You haven't told me much about yourself, but from what you have said, I gather you haven't always had it easy, yourself. But for whatever reason, you seem to be a pretty sensitive and caring sort of guy. One of those types who tries hard not to show it—but it shows through anyhow. And it shows, too, that you're learning how wrong all those old ideas in your head have been. You're learning that people we work with every day in the Valley aren't so much different than we are. Just different circumstances. . . different luck. . . different in ways that may be so slight it's frightening to think how close we really are to them. . . ."

I was nodding slowly because understanding was coming. I was amazed at his perceptiveness. He had me pegged. Inside, I've always known I had a soft streak a mile wide—but I'd worked hard all my life to keep it hidden.

"Y'know, Boot, I grew up down there in the South Valley."

"I know. I'd heard that. What made the difference for you?" I wasn't being nosy. I was interested.

"I don't know. Luck, maybe. Strong mother, maybe. Maybe a high school counselor who helped me join the Navy just at the right time. Maybe stumbling into medical corpsman school instead of becoming just a Seaman. I don't know.

"And, then again, maybe it was God."

I sat down on the old kitchen chair. Bryan was heavy.

Captain Meaker put the piece of painted wood on the bench and wiped red paint from his fingers onto his old pants. "Y'know, Booter, I think I owe you an apology, too."

"For what?"

"For the way we sort of forced you into prayers at the station. Thinking about it now, I can see that we put you into a mighty awkward position. It'd be pretty hard to be a 'boot' and have to say no to the others in your station house. We really don't have a right to impose that on you. Sometimes, when I don't stop to think, I become a really insensitive clod."

"Well," I stammered, "it *did* take a little to get used to it."

He nodded his understanding then stood up straight. "I'll tell you what," he said quietly. "From now on we'll go into the bunk room for our prayers."

This whole conversation was catching me by surprise. After all, Dad and so many other people had told me so often that the Mormons were out to catch my soul that I was having trouble believing what I was hearing. To my surprise, I found myself saying, "No, don't do that. I. . . well, I kind of. . . I've kind of gotten used to it. In fact, I kind of like it. It seems to start the day off right. . . and it's . . . well, it's *comforting* in a way." I knew what I wanted to say, but I couldn't think of the words I wanted, so I just shrugged and added, "It's just that it's a little *different* for me. That's all."

The captain smiled. "Well, good," he said, quietly. "It's supposed to be comforting. That's the whole idea behind prayer."

There was another moment of silence, then I ventured, "I guess I was wrong about you Mormons."

Captain Meaker raised his eyebrows.

"You know," I blundered on, "y'hear all those stories about how the only thing Mormons have in mind is converting everyone else in the world. I kept expecting you all to try to baptize me in the shower or something. But, except for the prayers, you haven't said or done anything to put pressure on me."

"And we won't, either," he replied. "I firmly believe that each of us has to find his own personal relationship with God and unless someone asks me about it, I'm not going to presume to meddle in his spiritual life. All I'll say is that the Church is the best thing that ever happened to me or my family."

That surprised me. I knew that I was about to put my foot into it again, but I continued anyway. "But you're. . . you're a Negro," I blurted. "I always thought Mormons wouldn't let you into their church."

The captain nodded slowly. "A lot of people think that, but the truth is. . . ."

Just then he was interrupted by a knock on the door. I reached over and opened it to admit young David. "Dad, Mom says dinner's ready." He turned to me and added, "She said to tell you she's set an extra place and she'd like to have you stay and eat with us."

I stood up and set Bryan, who was almost asleep, on the floor. "No," I said, looking at my watch, "my mother is expecting me for supper, and my girl and I were going to a movie."

They kept urging me to stay, and I kept making excuses. But as the captain stood at the door with me he said, "Boot, grab me sometime when you're interested. I'll answer your question then."

We shook hands, and just as I turned to leave I remembered something. I ran through the snow to the car, grabbed the wedding invitation I'd been carrying around for a week or so, ran back to the door, and handed it to him.

"Thanks," he said.

"I hope you can make it." As I drove away, I knew I didn't care any more what my father might think about Black people at my wedding.

Chapter Twelve

I worked the Tuesday before Thanksgiving and the day after. But it was like being a stranger in my own house. Don, Luis, and Captain Meaker had all taken vacation time. Steve Carlson, a captain from the north side and a couple of floaters, men who have no home station, filled in for them. In the evenings I spent a lot of time waxing things. I waxed all of Engine 5, waxed woodwork all over the station, waxed floors, then waxed my car and Linda's.

"You sure are an industrious little fella," Captain Carlson laughed. "How about asking for Engine 34 if you ever decide to transfer out of here? Our station could use a good waxer."

I gave his offer serious thought that evening. Maybe if I'd get that transfer I could bring some peace back between my father and me.

The captain and the others were back on shift the following Monday, and Captain Carlson's remark still wandered through my head occasionally. I almost picked up the phone to call the Battalion Chief, but I didn't. Then, just about noon, the phone rang.

"Station five," I answered.

"Good morning, Five." I recognized the voice. It was one of the dispatchers. "Confirming—do you carry A-Triple-F or Protein in your foam tank?"

I knew she was asking if we carried protein based foam or the newer AFFF, Aqueous Film Forming Foam, in the tank nestled amidships above our pump. "A-Triple-F," I answered.

"Thank you." She hung up.

I was turning away from the phone, thoroughly puzzled, when I heard the tones. "Engine Five. Highway Patrol requests mutual aid at the railroad underpass in Southlake. The railroad underpass in Southlake. They have a tanker of solvent upside down. HazMat is running with you."

We were out the door in a few seconds. Don turned us south on the main highway out of the city. Southlake is a small town about fifteen miles out, in farming country that surrounds the city. Chemical spills can be very interesting and small town fire departments are rarely equipped to cope with them. Our department's Hazardous Materials Unit was responding along with us on a special call for help.

At the edge of the little town we encountered a roadblock. We were directed around the spill so we could approach it from the south with the wind to our backs. Don finally pulled to a stop beside a large van marked "Hazardous Materials Response Unit." Its crew was just finishing dressing out in the full-covering exposure suits that make HazMat men look like something from a science fiction movie. I looked past them and saw a ten-thousand gallon tanker upside down in a shallow pool of clear liquid.

Captain Meaker walked to a group of men standing beside a State Highway Patrol car. He began to talk with a man who wore a white chief's helmet and a black coat with reflective lettering on the back that spelled out, "Southlake VFD." I walked up just in time to hear the volunteer chief say, ". . . We blocked the storm drains with sandbags. I was afraid of what might happen if that stuff got into the sewer system." Then he turned to Captain Meaker. "Will you rig out your foam equipment and stand by? All we have is protein and the book calls for A-Triple-F on this stuff."

All we had to do was change to a foam nozzle on the end of our hose. I was doing that when the captain shook his head, "These volunteers. . .! Their chief knew he could have houses full of explosive fumes if that stuff came up through sewer drains. . . so what did they do? They waded right in and plugged the drains! I haven't quite figured out whether volunteers are fools or heroes." He went on as if musing to himself, "Heroes, I guess. We have everything we need to work with. . . but these guys have nothing but bare hands. I guess you do what you have to do."

I nodded, watching a couple of volunteers who were standing in a stream of water while other firefighters hosed the chemical off their boots. You'd never catch me wading into something like that. One spark and you'd be all gone.

. . . .

The wind was bitterly cold. With our nozzle ready, Luis and I stood by to cover the HazMat men as they waded into the pool to try to plug the small hole in the tanker.

The HazMat captain gave us a signal. We covered the spill with a layer of AFFF. Then the three men in sealed protective suits waded into the puddle. There was something about the idea of wading through even a foamed flammable liquid that made my skin crawl.

I looked around. Don was standing beside the pump panel, warming his hands near the exhaust pipe. Captain Meaker was with the volunteer chief. I watched the HazMat crew as they slowly applied a long belt and a plug assembly around the large tank trailer and snugged it up. The flow of liquid stopped and they waded out of the pool.

The wind was cutting through me. I shivered. "What now?" I asked.

"We stand by until this mess is pumped up."

"How long?"

Luis shrugged. "Who knows? All night, sometimes."

The volunteers were hosing off the HazMat crew's boots. My thoughts began to wander away from the flooded underpass. "Luis?" I ventured.

"What?"

"You said one time that you'd tell me about Captain Meaker."

He nodded. "Whatta ya want'a hear?"

I shrugged. "Whatever you have to tell, I guess."

He shivered. "The main thing I have to tell is that I wish I'd worn my jacket under my turnout coat, that's what."

I laughed. I was wishing the same thing. But just then the HazMat captain came up behind us with a Highway Patrol lieutenant. "You guys might as well stand down, now. We're clear. Leave your hose rigged and get warm someplace."

We nodded gratefully. The lieutenant said, "You can use my patrol car over there."

Luis followed me into the car. I turned the heater blower up as high as it would go. We sat quietly for a few minutes then Luis said, "So you finally want to hear about the captain, huh?"

I nodded and waited for him to continue. Don was sitting in the cab of Engine 5 and the captain was sitting with the volunteer chief in another car.

"Captain Meaker," Luis said idly. "Well, Booter, if you haven't figured it out for yourself already, our cap is a different sort of guy." Luis was quiet again and I could tell he was collecting his thoughts.

A distant voice rattled from the police radio. Luis turned toward me. "Have you started to change your mind about our 'nigger' captain?"

I nodded.

"Good. 'Cause like I told you, you'll never find a finer man anyplace. You already owe him your life after that church. . . .

"Let's see. What can I tell you? He grew up down in the South Valley. Medical corpsman with a Marine combat unit in Vietnam. Somebody told me he won the Congressional Medal of Honor and two Purple Hearts over there. I don't know for sure. . . he never talks about it.

"First Black captain on the department. . . in fact, one of the first Black firefighters. He sort of paved the way for a lot of us. . . a lot of us *minorities*. He had some real problems at first, I hear. Things like little black ape dolls in his bed. Signs on his locker. Silent treatment. . . .

"Most people would'a quit, I think. But he hung on. Then, one day, he showed 'em all how wrong they'd been."

Luis unwrapped a Lifesaver and offered one to me. "Had a big warehouse light up one afternoon. One of those deals where there was lots of smoke and heat, but nobody could find the fire. A ladder crew was inside on a tag line when they got lost. Tag line burned off behind them. They couldn't find daylight.

"Meaker went back in again and again. Other people couldn't take the heat and kept backing out. They were just throwing water into the dark and all they were doing was making a lot of steam. Meaker used four bottles of air.

"He didn't find them. Just by luck somebody forced a big overhead door and found the men sitting right inside it. They were buddy breathing the last of their air when they got to 'em.

"Even though he didn't actually find the men, Meaker showed everyone that even a 'nigger' could be a good fireman."

Luis looked out the window. It was starting to snow. His voice was quieter when he continued. "He paved the way for a lot of us, like I said. I guess once they saw a jigaboo could be a fireman they decided even a Mexican could make it."

We sat and listened to the traffic on the police radio. I wanted to say something but I couldn't think of a way to put my thoughts into words.

"You met his family," Luis went on. "Three little foster children and three of his own. They often have more children than that. When things started to get crowded a couple of years ago, he just added another bedroom or two. He and Ellen take the children no one else wants. Retarded, crippled, mixed breeds, some fresh out of juvenile hall. . . .

"And, do you know what he does with his spare time? He volunteers as a teacher's aid at the school at the end of Dyer. Teaches reading, math, whatever else he can do. He says education is the way out for those kids. And it is, y'know?

"No working someplace on his off days, so Ellen has to have a part time job to make ends meet." Luis shook his head. "I don't think I could do what he's doing, . . . or what he's done, for that matter."

The radio voice was talking about an injury accident someplace. We stopped to listen.

"He could have been a Battalion Chief a long time ago. He passed the tests and he's come up on the lists time after time. But he turns it down. Says that wouldn't leave him enough time to do the other things he thinks he needs to do. . . like working with the kids at the school.

"And he's become a well-respected man in the city. Serves on special committees right and left. He was chairman of the Mayor's select committee to recommend improvements in the South Valley. Now he's fighting political battles to push those recommendations into realities. He's on the board of directors of the Boy's Clubs. Twice he's been a candidate for the school board but hasn't made it. Let's see. . . what else can I tell you?"

"What about him being a Mormon?" I asked. "Like I said before, I thought Black people couldn't join that church."

Luis smiled. "Black people sounds a lot better coming from you than what you called Meaker before." He nodded and went on. "Blacks have always been able to join the Church. They just can't hold the Priesthood. Y'see, all the men except Blacks hold the Priesthood. It's sort of a do-it-yourself church. We don't have any paid priests or ministers."

"But if he can't be a priest, why does he still belong?"

Luis shook his head. "That's something only he can answer. I've asked him, but he seems to have trouble explaining it." He paused. "I guess it's just something that comes from the heart. . . and how do you define something that comes from the heart? All I know is that I'm mighty glad he's what he is because he opened the door to the Church for me."

"For you?"

"Yep. I was raised a good Catholic Mexican until I met Dave Meaker. He made a fireman and a Mormon out of me!"

"Really?"

Luis nodded. I was just about to ask him how it happened when a knock on the window startled me. I looked out to see one of the volunteers. I rolled the window down. "Our wives have brought sandwiches and hot coffee. C'mon and get some."

I was starved. We crawled out of the patrol car and walked to the back of a station wagon where a couple of women were dispensing wrapped sandwiches and steaming cups. "Roast beef, chicken, or tuna?"

I took a roast beef and a chicken sandwich. "Coffee?" the woman asked Luis.

He grinned, "No coffee, thanks. I'm a good little Mormon boy. Do you have hot chocolate?"

She nodded and handed him a cup of hot water and a packet of chocolate. I don't know what possessed me, but when she asked me I said, "Me, too. I'll have chocolate."

Chapter Thirteen

The days just before our wedding were wild. Linda and my mother and her mother were running helter-skelter all over town on final arrangements. My father gradually thawed until we were on speaking terms again. Ours is a big Polish family with relatives all over creation, and they began gathering the day before the main event.

Uncle Stan and Aunt Sophie were first to arrive. Then came Uncle Joe and his wife and four kids, all under the age of ten and all equipped with voices that would drown out both Engine 5's siren and its horns. Next came Aunt Marie who hates the sight of Uncle Stan. A little after lunch my cousin Richard arrived with his new wife. Then Uncle Bertscha brought in his wife and my grandmother who is hard of hearing. As soon as Babushka, which is Polish for Grandma, got there the noise level went up as everyone shouted so she could understand.

There were more—many more. By the time we finished supper the house was crammed so full there was no room to sit down. My mother takes it as a personal insult if anyone wants to stay at a motel when they visit us, so the whole mob was packed wall to wall. Kids were supposed to sleep in the basement, women upstairs, men downstairs.

The kids giggled and chased each other all night. The women sat and gossiped until well after midnight. Uncle Stan and Uncle Bertscha had brought copious supplies of Schnapz and Vodka to add to my father's stash. By nine o'clock all the men were in that state of euphoria that only a well-potted Pole can reach. The place was a mad house.

I stayed sober, much to the consternation of Uncle Stan, who kept trying to push a glass into my hand. In fact I hadn't had a drink since the afternoon I'd gone to talk with Captain Meaker.

The wedding was scheduled for nine o'clock in the morning because December is a popular time for weddings, and the priests had something like twenty of them to perform that day. We'd been cautioned not to be late.

But nobody woke up until Babushka started yelling at about 7:30. Things went downhill from there.

Kids were being dragged this way and that by their mothers. Upstairs in the bathroom women were washing and dressing and making up and doing whatever else women do. Men were crowded around the kitchen sink, all trying to shave at the same time. Babushka kept yelling in Polish, "Hurry, all of you, or we'll be late!"

Uncle Stan decided some Vodka would help his headache. When the other uncles saw that they decided a sip or two would help theirs, too.

I don't know how we did it, but we all spilled out the doors into the waiting cars at precisely 8:45. Uncle Stan spilled out, too, and had to be picked up and carried under the arms by my father and Uncle Carl.

It's usually a twenty minute drive to St. Stephanie's but we made it in ten. Linda and her family were waiting anxiously in the Bingo hall.

Nine o'clock came. And went.

Nine-fifteen came. And went.

Nine-thirty came. And it went, too.

About nine forty-five a priest wandered into the Bingo hall. Linda's father collared him. "Yes," the priest said blandly in response to frantic questioning, "we're running a little late this morning. We'll call you when we're ready."

The hall was full of guests. Since I didn't know most of them, I decided they must belong to some of the other weddings scheduled that day. I wondered if anyone we knew would be in the church when our turn finally came.

I saw Luis and his wife off in a corner with Don and his wife, but I couldn't get to them through the crowd. Just then my father nudged me and pointed toward the stage. "What's *he* doing here?" he demanded, pointing to Captain Meaker.

I wilted inside but I said, "I invited him."

"You invited *him?*"

"I work with him, don't I?"

My father grunted with disgust. Then Uncle Bertscha distracted him, and I was able to get away.

Around ten, a young priest came into the room and shouted for quiet. Then he asked, "Is this the Nichols-McKinney wedding?"

I shook my head. Someone shouted, "No, it's not."

The young priest started out, shaking his head in bewilderment. Babushka caught him by the arm and began shouting at him in a mixture of Polish and English. The priest didn't look as if he knew what she was saying, but he must've known she wasn't happy.

"I'll try. I'll try," he kept repeating.

About ten-thirty someone finally called our names and invited all our guests into the church. The room was almost empty when they'd gone.

A moment later the young priest returned. "I guess we're ready," he said. "Who's supposed to perform the ceremony?"

"Father Lambert," I answered.

The young priest looked perplexed. "Oh, dear," he said. "I don't know if he can."

"Why not?" my father asked.

"Well," hedged the cleric, "he's . . .uh, . . . he's not in the best of health right now."

My father and I nodded. We both knew Father Lambert quite well.

The young priest escorted us up the stairs to the back of the sanctuary where he left us for a moment. Then he returned to tell us, "Father Lambert isn't available. Father Rodriguez will do the ceremony."

My father bristled. "That *Mexican?*" he asked.

"Dad!" I hissed.

The young priest peeked through the door. "Look in there," he whispered. "Do we have the right guests there for your wedding?"

I peered through the opening. I recognized several people so I said, "Looks like it."

The young man sighed with relief.

Just then the organ began playing, the door opened and I felt myself being shoved into the aisle. I walked with my father down to where my brother, Andy, who was my best man, and the others were waiting. My sister and her family stood behind my mother. My mother was already bawling into a pink handkerchief as she watched me, her youngest baby, getting ready to fly from the nest.

The organ shifted gears. The familiar wedding march started. I looked up and caught my breath. Linda, holding her father's arm, was making her way slowly down the aisle. She was beautiful!

They arrived at the altar. We all lined up with our backs to the crowd. I smiled when I noticed that Linda's hands were shaking so badly her bouquet was shedding its petals.

We faced the altar and waited. No priest.

We waited some more. No priest.

I studied the statuary above the High Altar carefully. Still no priest.

Linda was still shaking. My father was beginning to mutter obscene things under his breath. No priest.

I began wishing I'd had some of Uncle Stan's Vodka. He was sleeping peacefully in the second row right behind my mother.

The organist had just started another round of Lohengrin when a small door beside the choir seats opened and a priest I'd never seen before walked in, adjusting his vestments. He stepped briskly over to us, said something to the altar boy and turned to us.

"Good morning, John and Laurie," he said.

"We're not John and Laurie," I whispered and told him our names. He looked confused. "Isn't this the Nichols-McKinney wedding?"

I shook my head.

"Oh, hell!" he muttered. "Who are you, then?"

I told him.

"You have the license and all?"

I nodded.

He paused. "Might as well do it," he said. "You're all ready."

He began the wedding Mass. It seemed to go on and on. Except for calling us John and Laurie several times he got through it as quickly as he could. Finally, he pronounced us man and wife. "You may kiss your bride," he said. Then he whispered loudly, "And for Pete's sake, hurry! I've got weddings stacked up from now 'til tomorrow!"

Linda's father had rented a big hall for the reception. It was crowded. A band was playing. People were visiting, eating, and drinking. Poles and Slovenians can drink like no others, except maybe the Irish. So, with Linda's Irish relations and my Polshskis at work, the liquor flowed freely.

The receiving line was ten miles long. By the time everyone had wended through it my hand was sore from the men's handshakes, and I was sure my cheek was blistered from the women's kisses. I was proud of my father because he kept his tongue quiet when Luis and Captain Meaker brought their wives through the line.

After the receiving line ordeal, the dancing really began to get serious. Waltzes alternated with polkas. Then the band swung into an Irish jig and back to a polka. Linda and I danced until neither of us had any breath left, then we went to admire the collection of wedding gifts piled on tables along the side of the hall.

Luis found me there. He whispered that he had something special for me. "I know you don't have any vacation time yet," he said. "so I got you some extra time. Bill Harvey from Engine Six owes me some time for when I doubled back for him, so he's going to double for you next shift. That'll give you a longer honeymoon!"

I was grateful.

Captain Meaker caught up with me at the liquor table. I poured him a glass of Sprite while he told me, "Hey, Boot. I know you don't have any vacation coming yet so I talked Bud Tucker into paying some time he owes me by working for you. You can take the next shift off!"

I was grateful. The way my head felt right then, I'd need all the time off I could get. I told the captain about Luis's offer. He laughed. "Okay, then, so take the next two shifts off. We've got you covered!"

Just then my father wandered over. He was stewed to the gills. When he gets that way, he can be belligerent. I started to worry.

"This your captain?" he asked.

I nodded and introduced Captain Meaker.

Dad regarded the captain for a moment before he asked suddenly, "Ain't you a little dark to be a officer in th' fire department? Or in anything else for that matter?"

I cringed, but Captain Meaker laughed. "No," he answered. "Actually, it comes in handy now and then. Like when I've pulled a boneheaded blunder and the Battalion Chief is looking for me. Then I can just blend in with the smoke!"

Dad regarded the captain silently for a moment longer before he muttered something uncomplimentary under his breath and staggered off.

"I'm sorry," I apologized. "He's not very nice when he's sober, either."

Captain Meaker shook his head. "Don't worry, Booter. It stopped getting to me a long time ago."

We stood and talked some more until Uncle Bertscha drifted over and began trying to get the captain to dance with him. I steered my uncle back to his wife. While I was doing that, I noticed Captain Meaker, Luis, and Don, with their wives, heading out the door.

. . . .

Linda and I finally managed to slip away much later in the afternoon. The car had been appropriately decorated and some screwball had wired the brake lights into the horn. That took a few minutes to figure out and fix, but we were finally on our way out of the city to the mountain ski resort where we were going to spend a few days—thanks in part to the captain and Luis.

We ate at the best steak house in the little mountain town then headed for the best motel I'd been able to afford. We were worn out and decided that perhaps a little time in the Jacuzzi would perk us up. Instead, the warm circulating water nearly put us both to sleep. We stumbled back to our room about nine. I was so tired I kept falling asleep while I waited for Linda to brush her teeth.

The rest of the night wasn't too memorable except for the time around one in the morning when somebody started a car outside and turned the headlights through our window. When the room suddenly flooded with light, my firehouse reflexes took over. I leaped out of bed, crashed against the bedside table, and was stumbling around looking for my boots and bunker pants when Linda asked sleepily, "What on earth are you *doing?*"

. . . .

We slept most of the morning, skied a little that afternoon, enjoyed a great dinner that we finally were awake enough to taste, Jacuzzied and Saunaed, called room service and watched a good movie. Things worked a whole lot better that night than the night before.

Chapter Fourteen

The days between our wedding and Christmas passed quickly. A-shift drew duty on Christmas day—a day I don't think I'll ever forget.

I was replacing a broken pulley at the top of the hose-drying tower when the tones came in the first time. It took several seconds to scramble down and into the engine bay. I heard the dispatcher saying, "Engine Five, an EMS call. 2460 South MacAllen. 2460 South MacAllen. Unknown medical problems. Use caution, the police are running with you. Engine Five, use channel three."

Twenty-four sixty South MacAllen was a small, neat house in a decaying neighborhood not far from the highrise ghetto. Don stopped in front of the house. I grabbed the first aid equipment and followed Luis up the sidewalk to the door. Captain Meaker was already on the front porch. He stood with both hands on the shoulders of an old man who cried over and over, "I shot her! I shot her! I didn't mean to! Oh, my God, I didn't mean to. . . ."

I followed Luis through the front door into the living room. He stopped so suddenly I ran into his back. I heard him catch his breath, then I saw the old woman.

She was sitting upright in an upholstered chair. Even from where I stood I could see that the whole top of her head was gone. A small red spot under her chin marked the bullet's entrance. Its exit was announced by crimson and pink that splattered and stained the ceiling.

I stood back. I thought my stomach had become accustomed to almost anything, but it was reeling around inside me. Luis must have been feeling shock at the sight, too, because for no reason I could see he walked over to the old woman and lifted her arm—feeling for a pulse.

A police officer came in. When he saw her, I heard him mutter something foul. Then he spoke into his radio, calling for the medical examiner.

I needed fresh air. I walked back onto the porch. Captain Meaker and Don had a blanket around the old man's shoulders. Don was sitting on a porch chair beside the old man, sort of holding him up while a police officer wrote on a note pad.

The old man was still repeating, "I didn't mean to... it was an accident. I bought it so we could protect ourselves. Kids from the Towers are always over here and sometimes they try to break in. And sometimes they follow us down the street. She was afraid... so I bought her the gun. It was our Christmas present... I was showing her how it worked...."

"What size was it?" asked the policeman.

The old man shook his head. "I don't know... I got a big one."

The other officer stood in the door behind me. The gun hung from a pencil stuck through the trigger guard. "Three fifty-seven magnum," he said flatly. "Loaded with hollow points."

The first police officer looked at the sobbing old man. "I'm sorry, sir," he said, "but I have to read you your rights." He pulled a small card from his pocket and began reading.

We stayed until the police had driven off with the old man. Then, with the medical examiner's permission, we headed back toward Station 5.

. . . .

We hadn't gone far when I heard our tones again, the dispatcher saying, "Engine Five, Engine Twenty-two, Ladder Twenty-two, Battalion Three. 3330 West San Juan Drive. 3330 West San Juan Drive. A residential fire. Use channel two."

I glanced at my watch. It was 10:17 in the morning.

I hadn't been wearing my helmet or flash hood, so I was putting them on when I heard Luis holler above the engine's noise, "We've got one cooking!"

I looked around and saw a boil of smoke looming up ahead of us. Then I heard the captain's voice coming back through the speaker. "Dispatch, Engine Five. We have a single story, single family residence. Fire is showing at the front. Ask Engine Twenty-two to lay in behind us."

Flames were rolling out a front window as we jerked to a stop in the street in front of the house. Engine 22 would bring us a hose from the hydrant. We would work with water from the seven hundred-fifty gallons in our on-board tank. I grabbed my breathing apparatus, pulled the nozzle of the Mattydale and headed for the front door with Luis right behind me. The captain stopped me. "Go around back!" he yelled. "It's only in the front room!"

We dragged the hose around the side of the house and pushed through the kitchen door, attacking from the unburned portion. Luis and I dragged the hose, crouching low under the smoke, while Captain Meaker began searching rooms. The living room was a mass of rolling flame. Tongues of it licked through the hall to nearly as far as the kitchen.

I led the way into the hall, opened the nozzle, and began pushing the fire back on itself. It was black in just a few seconds. We went on through the front door and onto the porch, getting there just as Engine 22 pulled up behind Engine 5 with the supply hose.

We backed through the house again, mopping out hot spots as we went. Ladder 22's crew came in with the Battalion 3 Chief, Chief Halvorsen. They began pulling wall and ceiling material off in the living room and hallway, looking for fire extension.

Captain Meaker and Chief Halvorsen were looking at something in the corner of the room. It was the charred skeleton of a Christmas tree. The chief was saying, "Here's the point of origin. See how the carbon's burned clean off the wall behind it? Burn goes all the way to the floor here, too."

Captain Meaker disagreed. "I think it started in the chair beside the tree. See how deeply charred this cushion is? Looks like a cigarette did it. The tree finally caught and burned so hot it cleaned the carbon off the wall."

"Well," the chief said, "I guess the fire investigators can figure it out." He paused and poked at the remains of a family's Christmas located around the base of the burned tree and added, "Look at this. Little kids' toys. Isn't that pathetic?"

There was a small commotion at the door. I turned and saw Engine 22's captain leading a man and woman into the room. The woman was crying. The man looked stricken. Two small children stared into the room behind them, kept from entering by a firefighter with "L22" on the side of his helmet. They shook their heads and talked in Spanish. Then the man said to me in English, a tone of pure despair in his voice, "It was all we had. In here, it was all we had. . . ."

I nodded and patted the man on the shoulder. He began to cry. I don't think I'll ever get used to things like that.

A moment later Engine Twenty-two's engineer shoved his helmet in front of me. I pulled my wallet out and dropped in all the money I had with me.

. . . .

The tones came again about one in the afternoon. We'd just finished eating lunch and were settling down to watch a Christmas special. "Engine Five," she said, "Engine Five, an EMS call. 2862 Dyer, Apartment 216. 2862 Dyer, Apartment 216. Report of a drowning. Use channel three."

Christmas traffic was relatively light. Don wound us over to the highrise ghetto in near-record time while I wondered how in the world anyone could drown in a second floor apartment. I had the answer soon enough.

Elevators are slow in the ghetto buildings, so we ran up the stairs. Just as we topped out at the second floor, I could see a knot of people gathered in the hall ahead. They parted quickly to let us through. Outside a door with "216" painted on it was a woman crying in the arms of another woman who held her tightly.

Inside the apartment we found two boys, both about fifteen or so, who were bent double over a baby on the floor. One of them was puffing into the baby's nose and mouth. Captain Meaker knelt beside them and when he had the Ambu Bag ready, he motioned them aside and began squeezing air into the baby from the bag's large, flexible air bellows. I quickly hooked a line from the oxygen tank to a tab on the end of the bag so the baby was getting a high concentration of oxygen.

"Do you want paramedics?" I asked the captain.

He nodded, so I reached to pull the portable radio from its pocket on the front of his coat. "Dispatch, Engine Five. Send paramedics to this location. We have an infant in respiratory arrest."

"Cardiac, too," Luis told me.

"Dispatch, the baby is full Code Blue. It's in cardiac arrest, too."

More tones and a paramedic unit was on its way. Because of the high number of false alarms from South Valley, I knew that dispatchers rarely sent paramedic units on the first call. Paramedic units are too valuable to be running all over the city on wild goose calls.

Luis was working the baby's chest with two fingers. "He's a little big for that," the captain said. "Use three or four fingers. Get a little more depression on the sternum."

I guessed the baby was almost two. I could hear his mother in the hall. She was gasping, "I didn't leave him for long. The phone rang and I went an' answered it. It was my mother sayin' 'Merry Christmas' and we talked a little. An' when I went back in he was floatin' in the water. He could always sit up so good, before. I thought he'd be okay. . . ."

I was thinking malevolent thoughts about the mother's intelligence when a police officer pushed his way into the room. "Paramedics are right behind me," he said.

They were setting up their equipment on the run, ready to go the instant they hit the floor. They stuck electrodes onto the child's chest and turned on the monitor. "Straight line," one of them observed. The other spoke into the radio while the captain and Luis kept pumping.

The paddles were ready. A low-wattage shock hit the little boy's body. It convulsed. The line flicked upward for a second then flattened again. "Hit him again." I knew they were just putting on a show for the public. Straight lines on the monitor don't react in real life as they do on television. But the public expects the paddles and the shocks, so the medics give it to them. It avoids nasty accusations and lawsuits later.

Second and third shocks did nothing. Finally the paramedics rocked back on their heels and signalled the captain and Luis to stop. A doctor's voice from the radio confirmed the paramedics' actions and the little life was ended.

"Bathtub drowning?" asked one of the paramedics.

I nodded. He shook his head. "Second one today. We just got off one in the University Hills."

From one of the most wealthy to one of the poorest sections of the city. I took back my thoughts about the mother and decided it could happen to anyone. Then I bit my tongue. I'd told myself that from me there'd be no more comparisons between the north and south sides of the freeway—but it was a tough resolve to follow.

I stood and watched the medics wrap the baby in a small, white sheet. I don't know whether it was the day—Christmas and all—but a sudden, huge lump rose into my throat and I was having trouble seeing. I sort of sagged back against the wall. I was leaning there when an elderly Black woman touched my arm. "Bless you," she said. "Thank you for trying."

I stumbled through the door, down the hall, and out to the tailboard of Engine 5 where I sat with my head in my hands fighting for control.

. . . .

We didn't run any more that day or night. When I got home the next morning, Linda asked, "How was your Christmas?"

It was a hard question to answer.

Chapter Fifteen

December rolled into January. Linda and I had our first big fight because one day she washed my helmet. You just don't wash a firefighter's helmet! We pride ourselves in all the dirt and soot and scorch on our helmets and I'd worked hard and had endured a lot of smoke and heat to make my helmet as macho as I could. And she went and washed it all away! That's like stealing merit badges from a Boy Scout! Worse, even. . . .

She nervously sallied forth to begin her student teaching, and for the first time I saw large-scale dying.

It was bitterly cold that night, and the wind was whistling straight down out of the Yukon. On nights like that old furnaces, in the crowded little wooden houses of the South Valley, start to come unglued. We get a lot of calls for gas leaks. It's usually a pilot light blown out by a gust of wind coming down the chimney. The gas company charges money for a callout—the fire department doesn't. So people who don't know how to light a pilot light call us and claim they smell gas. We ventilate and relight the pilot, and everyone is happy.

We'd been out on pilot light calls all afternoon and well into the evening. I was tired, so I dropped into bed a little early. I vaguely heard Don and Luis come into the bunk room, and suddenly I was wide awake. A dispatcher had hit the magic button that turns on our lights. As the room filled with brightness, I rolled out of bed. My feet automatically found my boots with my bunker pants nested around them. I was pulling them up when the dispatcher's voice began sounding out the alarm.

Don sat on the side of his bed in his strange underwear, copying the address onto one of his run cards while Luis and I headed out the door, down the hall, and into the engine bay. The police were reporting a fire in one of the wooden apartment houses about three blocks from Station 5.

I was just pulling my flash hood over my head when Don clambered into the cab. He started the engine. We waited for the captain. We waited some more and he still didn't appear. Don hit the Traffic Blaster and its blast rattled the building. Still no captain.

Luis reached across the engine cover and hit me on the arm. He shouted, "He's got the pillow over his head again. Go get him!"

I jumped off the Engine and hurried up the hall to the captain's private room. I banged the door open and could see him curled up with the pillow pulled over his head. I grinned and kicked the bed, jerking the pillow off at the same time. His eyes popped open and he looked up at me, open-mouthed. "Hey," I hollered, "people are dying out there and you're sleeping like a baby. . . d'you want to go with us?"

I'd regret that crack later.

The captain hit the floor, jerked his bunkers up and stumbled down the hall behind me. "Does Don have the run?"

"Yep," I answered, laughing.

I scrambled back into my seat while the captain pulled on his coat and climbed into the cab. Don rolled us into the street, turned right, and hit the accelerator.

I heard the dispatcher call for confirmation that we were running. I knew they only did that when a unit was late to acknowledge, and they wanted to confirm that nothing was wrong with the equipment and that the unit heard the call. "Engine Five, acknowledge."

I heard the captain's voice over the speaker, "Engine Five, acknowledging."

Then I heard the dispatcher's voice again with a message that made my skin crawl. "Engine Five and all units responding to LaCrosse Street, police advise fire in the hallways and people are starting to jump."

I felt the Engine lurch forward as Don's foot hit the floor metal.

. . . .

We slid around a corner and stopped abruptly. "Take the hydrant!" the captain shouted. I tumbled off, grabbed the hose and my hydrant wrench, and looked ahead. Fire was rolling from several front windows of a four- or five-story apartment building. I reached up, without orders, and grabbed a second hose to lay doubles for a better water supply.

I snagged the hydrant in record time and ran the half block to where Don had spotted Engine 5 in the middle of the street. There were no other pieces of apparatus in sight. Despite our late departure, we were still first on the scene. One of our hoses lay snaked from the Engine through the front door. Luis and Captain Meaker had already made entry.

I looked up and almost stopped moving. The windows were filled with people. People were hanging from practically every opening in the wall. They were waving and screaming while smoke boiled from the windows over their heads.

I yanked my breathing apparatus from its compartment. I was slinging it on when Don came up. "Cap says he wants you to ladder for rescue. Go for the third floor first!"

That puzzled me for a second until I remembered an instructor mentioning the order of rescue in situations like these. Jumpers from a second floor will probably survive. Jumpers from a third floor onto a concrete sidewalk will probably die. Rescue on a fourth floor takes too much time with a hand ladder even if the ladder will reach that high. And, above a fourth floor—a Ladder company is needed. We save as many as we can. As for the others. . . well. . . maybe we pray if we have time and breath to spare.

Rounding the corner of the Engine, I saw a baby falling through the air. I faltered until I saw a police officer catch the baby and set it quickly on the sidewalk so he could catch the next one—already on the way down.

Don helped me pull the ladder from its mount and carry it to the building. We were setting it up when I saw the black smoke billowing from a fourth floor window suddenly flash into flame as its unburned carbon and gases reached ignition temperature. The man who had been in the window scrambled out and fell, head first, toward the pavement. Instinctively, I started toward him to try a catch. Don caught my arm and held me back. The man hit with a heavy whump and lay writhing on the sidewalk. Another window lit up. I saw three figures come out of that one.

We spotted the ladder at a window. Don shouted, "Go! Go!" He slipped under and held the rungs, heeling the ladder so it wouldn't slip out from under me. I realized that he was violating a vital Departmental policy: he was an engineer away from his pump panel while firefighters using his hoses were inside a burning building. Luis and Captain Meaker were on their own.

Don held the ladder with one hand while I started up. He had his radio in the other hand. "Dispatch, Engine Five," he said. "Give us third and fourth alarms on this one and 'special call' some extra ladders."

I was about halfway up the ladder when I realized my air mask wasn't in place. Smoke was heavy. I started to cough, but there was no time to pull the mask on now. I reached the window and found a young woman with a cat in her arms. Before I could do anything, she handed me the cat and started clambering out the window. The cat promptly came uncorked and began slashing at me with its claws. I dropped it. "Land on your feet, pussycat!" I shouted after it.

Funny how your mind works in tight spots. For me it seemed to switch into slow motion so that everything—even the tiniest details—stood out.

I got the woman out facing the ladder and walked her down in front of me. "Is anyone else in there?" I shouted.

"No, man. I was all alone!"

I helped her from the last rung and turned around. Another Engine company was in the street beside Engine 5. Its crew was pulling a hose through the front door to help Captain Meaker and Luis. Two policemen were trying to pull its ladder off.

Don and I walked the ladder to another window. He set it into place while I took a moment to pull my mask on. I wasn't worried too much about toxic smoke, but I didn't want to get caught in a flashover without it. A firefighter can take a lot of heat with full gear on—even a fireball rolling past when smoke suddenly flashes.

Three people, a woman and two men, came down the ladder with me that time. Ladder 18 was in the street in front of Engine 5. It's not really a ladder at all, but an aerial platform—"cherrypicker," some people call them. The two men in the bucket were slowly trying to weave their way upward through the maze of wires and cables strung from poles along the street. One touch with the high-voltage lines and it could be all over for them.

You'd think the fire department would be able to call the electric company and have the power shut off in the area of a fire. But it doesn't work that way. Firefighters have to work between and around the wires. It would cost too much for electric companies to install isolation switches that would allow cutting power to a block of buildings. I guess firefighters are less expensive.

More Engine and Ladder companies were arriving and setting up. More ladders were sprouting. Hand ladders extended from the sidewalk to the second and third floors. Two platforms and an aerial ladder were working on the fourth and fifth floors. But it looked like most of the people on the fifth floor had been beyond help. The top floor had flashed and flame rolled from most of the windows up there. Ambulance crews were on the sidewalk checking the jumpers, trying to help those they could. People who hadn't jumped had disappeared from the windows.

I was scrambling back up the ladder when I looked up. A boy was leaning out the fourth floor window directly above the window my ladder reached. He was screaming to me as smoke billowed around him. Then I saw the first flashes of fire in the smoke that surrounded him. When the smoke lit up he popped out the window like a cork from a gun. His hair and shirt were on fire as he fell toward me. I grabbed the ladder as tightly as I could with my right hand and got my left ready to try a catch. He hit the ladder about three rungs above me and slid right down into my arms.

The impact nearly knocked me off the ladder. Then, as the boy began to roll off the left side, I grabbed him. The ladder began to twist sideways. I hung on, ready for the ride down, when it suddenly twisted back again. Looking up, I saw that a man in the window above had grabbed the top rung and was pulling it back. I pulled the boy close and used the front of my coat to smother flames on the front of his shirt while I slapped at flames in his hair. Fire flashed up past my face. I was very glad I'd taken time to pull my mask on.

Someone on the ground saw us and turned water on the boy.

By the time I reached the bottom of the ladder, two people above me were climbing down without help. A Battalion Chief took the boy. Another fireman, who had taken Don's place under the ladder helped me move it to another window.

Smoke was starting to go white as hoses inside turned the heat to steam. Within a few minutes, steam was pouring out all over. A Bat Chief with a bullhorn ordered us off the ladders and to an interior rescue effort.

I teamed on with two men from Ladder 12. We started up the stairs with orders to search out the third floor. We met Captain Meaker and Luis coming down. It struck me that their bells weren't ringing. This whole thing had taken less than the fifteen to twenty minutes it takes to run through a tank of air!

As they passed, I asked, "You guys okay?"

Luis nodded and Captain Meaker said, "Yeah. We're fine. But this one was a hot son-of-a-gun. Looks like somebody poured Diesel fuel up and down all the halls and stairways and touched it off. Must'a been mad at somebody in here."

Although the thought of that almost made me sick, I knew that it was really a common occurrence. I could see tell-tale black "trailers" on the stairs where the burning liquid had been.

I'd been wondering why the fire had gotten into the apartments so quickly. Why hadn't people simply closed their doors and shut the fire out? I found the answer when I turned a corner into one soot-blackened hall. Above each door was a transom. Most of the transoms were wide open.

Firefighters were already starting to lead shocked, terrified survivors down the halls from their homes.

. . . .

We searched through rooms by the wavering glow of our flashlights. It's kind of hard to separate a charred mattress from a charred body. The first time I found a body with its lips curled back and its white teeth grinning at me, I about lost my control.

We found two on the third floor. One of them had been about five years old.

WHEN THE BRAVE ONES CRIED

. . . .

Overhaul took a long time and daylight was starting to break when Don backed Engine 5 into the station. Captain Meaker had been very quiet and grim-faced throughout the long night. Now he went straight back to his room and closed the door behind him.

Don, Luis, and I cleaned equipment until **B**-shift arrived. They started helping while Don took Captain Harris aside and spoke to him for a second. Then they walked down the hall to the captains' room, knocked twice, and slipped inside.

I looked at Luis. He shrugged and asked simply, "How'd you feel if it was you?"

"But he didn't hold us up that long," I protested.

Luis shrugged again. "A minute, maybe. A lot can happen in a minute in a fire like that."

We cleaned in silence. Chief Halvorsen, our Bat Chief, came in. He went directly back to the captains' room. They were all still in there when I left the station.

Linda was gone when I got home, so I showered and tried unsuccessfully to get a little sleep. I puttered around the apartment all afternoon. I had supper ready by the time she got home. Full of enthusiasm for the teaching she was doing, she gave me a blow-by-blow report of every detail of her day.

I only half listened.

Television news that night set the toll at eight dead, eighteen badly injured, and about forty homeless. I was surprised there hadn't been more. At the time it had seemed like it.

"Wasn't that terrible?" Linda asked when a commercial came on.

"What?" I asked, lost in my thoughts.

"That fire."

I nodded absently. She looked at me. "Were you there?"

I stood up. "Yeah, I was there."

Then I went outside and took a walk. There are some things you can't talk about with anyone for awhile. They have to set a little before you can think about them.

Chapter Sixteen

Linda was bubbling over with her student teaching. She'd drawn an assignment in one of the city's better schools—a place in a fashionable neighborhood in the northeast foothills. Her supervising teacher was supposed to be one of the best in the city. Linda was sure putting her heart into her work.

She managed to pull me in, too. I cut and pasted and colored and glued. I lettered little alphabet cards and traced little zebras and alligators and mice and ducks and cows and lions and tigers. Our kitchen table looked like a zoo, barnyard, and circus all in one.

She told me every evening of her successes. She agonized over her failures. I found myself smiling with her when she told me of how little girls I'd never met had giggled when they saw my attempts at drawing a squirrel. And I listened with concern as she told me about Steven, a little boy whose mother was terribly disappointed with him because he wasn't catching on to reading as fast as the others.

"Reading?" I asked. "In *Kindergarten?*"

"Oh, yes. The parents out there are all doctors, lawyers, insurance executives. . . it's a matter of pride. They think their children should have been *born* reading Tolstoy."

I just shook my head.

She'd been after me to visit the class, so one day I talked Luis into going with me to tell the kids about firemen and firetrucks. I even arranged for a unit from Station 38 to go to the school.

Luis was waiting in the parking lot when I drove up. I waved to him. Suddenly it struck me that he and I had become pretty good friends. I shook my head and smiled as I realized how much I'd changed in just a few months.

We trooped into the building, both of us carrying our turnout gear in duffle bags. We found Linda's classroom and entered amid a sudden bubbling of excitement. We spent the next half hour going through the fire safety program ritual—Kindergarten variety.

The students responded with infectious enthusiasm. All except one little boy named Vincent. Vincent sat with a dour look throughout the whole thing. Each time one of us pulled something more from our bag of tricks, Vincent commented that his father had one to beat it. Vincent didn't want to try on a helmet because it was stupid. Vincent didn't want to stop, drop, and roll because he was wearing new pants. Vincent's father, he informed us, was chief of the whole fire department and owned three fire trucks, too.

I looked anxiously at my watch and then out the window. There they were. Ladder 38 was just parking in the school lot—right on time. We trooped outside with about five little kids holding my hands and five or six hanging on Luis. We were about halfway across the yard when suddenly the Ladder's engine roared, its lights kicked on and it drove out of the lot, turned left and disappeared down the street with its siren and blaster bringing people to their windows.

"Well, heck," Luis observed. "Don't you think they could have at least *waved?*"

A little girl who clung to my right hand asked, "Where did they go?"

"I don't know. I guess they had to go to a fire."

Vincent looked after them with disgust. "Well," he muttered, "*my* father would never break an appointment that way!"

Linda whispered to me, "Vincent's father moved out and filed for divorce a week ago."

We packed our gear back into our duffle bags and walked back to our cars. I was hungry. "Buy you lunch," I offered.

Luis grinned. "Thought you'd never ask. Y'know, there's an old fire department tradition that junior firefighters always buy for senior firefighters."

"Really?" I laughed. "How long's that tradition been around?"

"Oh, about thirty seconds."

Luis followed me to the restaurant of my choice. We ordered and walked to the salad bar. "Did you hear that two more people from the LaCrosse fire died?"

I said, "No. But I'm not surprised." Then, dabbing Russian dressing over my lettuce, I asked abruptly, "Luis, are they going to write up the captain?"

Luis shook his head. "No. That's not the kind of mistake the department writes up. We've all slept through alarms. I'm sure all the chiefs have, too. Besides, no write-up could be worse than what the captain's putting himself through."

As we began to eat another question that had been gnawing its way through me surfaced. I asked, "Luis, would you tell me about the Mormon church?"

He looked surprised. "Sure. But why? I thought you were a good Catholic."

"No," I said slowly. "Not any more. I don't know exactly what's wrong, but somehow I've lost all my feelings for it. Hard to put into words. . . . "

He nodded. "I think I understand."

"I thought you might. Since you said you used to be Catholic, too."

"Yeah. Yeah, I used to be." He picked at his salad for a moment. "So, what do you want to know?"

I realized I didn't even know enough to ask an intelligent question. I hedged by saying, "All of it, I guess."

"Got a week?" he smiled.

The waitress brought our lunches. While he cut his meat, Luis began telling me his story.

"I think I know how you feel," he began, "because that's the way I felt a few years ago. I'd been to parochial schools all the way through high school. I'd been an altar boy—the whole shot. But the older I grew, the more I came to realize that something was missing. I didn't know what it was, exactly, but it seemed empty, somehow. Like I'd go to church on Sunday and nothing would happen to me. Y'know what I mean?"

I nodded. I knew.

"I mean, we'd go through all the rituals and such. . . the priests would get up and do their thing. . . but it was all just *words*. . . and they seemed empty. Then you'd read in the papers that the Cardinals were arguing with the Pope and the Bishops were arguing with the Cardinals and the Priests were arguing with the Bishops and the people were confused.

"It was like give your offering, play your Bingo cards, say your confession and a few Hail Marys, mind your own business and get drunk on Friday. I figured there had to be more to it than that."

He paused to salt his potato. "I got married. She was from a family that hadn't been to church since she was christened. There was a baby coming."

He paused again and looked out the window. "Baby was born dead." He shrugged, spread his hands helplessly, and went on. "So we're arranging for the funeral when all of a sudden I realized that the baby hadn't been christened. I asked the priest, and he said that was too bad. . . nothing he could do. We just had to accept God's will. . . ."

Luis scowled and wrestled with a tough piece of meat. "I'd just gone to work under Dave Meaker at Station Five. He was always right there when we needed him. Heck, I'd hardly been in the station more than a week when we lost the baby and still didn't know him from Adam. But he was right there helping—and comforting."

He sighed. "His message was whole a lot more comforting that the priest's had been, too. It made good sense. He told us the church was wrong. Flat wrong. That little ones who die before what he called 'the age of accountability,' which is eight, *do* go on to Heaven instead of Purgatory. Somehow, that was just what we needed to hear right then. . . ."

I was quiet, hoping he'd go on. Finally Luis said, "He told us a lot of other things, too. And they all made sense. Good sense. The more I heard of his Mormon church, the more I liked what I heard.

"Anyhow, one thing led to another. Pretty soon we were going with him and Ellen on Sundays. Then the missionaries visited us and we joined. It was that simple."

I nodded. "But what do you believe in?"

"You want the crash course, huh?"

"I guess so."

He took a deep breath and began to tell me a story that seemed so farfetched to me the first time I heard it, my head spun.

Chapter Seventeen

January moved into February. Captain Meaker was awfully moody for a few weeks, but he finally got over it. He did ask us, though, to take a second on the way out of the bunk room to look into his room and be sure he was up.

Life, both at the station and at home, shifted into a steady routine. I began to become bored sitting around on my days off waiting for Linda to come home from school, so I started drifting down to my sister's husband's body shop to work on cars with him. That turned into a paying job when one of his body and paint men quit.

But there still wasn't enough in my life to keep me satisfied. You'd think that with a steady diet of action at work—auto accidents, fires, pilot light calls, EMS runs, the weekly meetings of the knife and gun society—you name it, we had it—I'd be satisfied. But something was missing, and I couldn't figure out what.

I couldn't sleep one night. I was flopping around in bed so much I woke Linda. "What's the matter?" she asked.

"Can't sleep," I growled.

She curled up closer. "Why?"

"I don't know. . ."

Some of the nameless misery I was feeling must have shown in my voice, because she said, "Something has been bothering you for weeks now. What is it?"

I tried to answer, but all I could get out was a lame, "I don't know. I just feel empty inside."

"About what?"

I shook my head in the dark. "I don't *know!*" I answered irritably. "It's not my job—I enjoy it. It's not the people I work with—I've really come to like them—no matter what my father may think of them. Goodness knows it isn't *you!* I just don't know what it is!"

I could feel her nodding her head. "Where did you get those little pamphlets?"

"What pamphlets?"

"The ones about the Mormon Church."

"Oh," I suddenly remembered. "Luis and I were talking that day we went to visit the school and he gave them to me. I put them down and never got back to reading them."

"They're very interesting," she said quietly. We lay silent for awhile. Then she added, "You know, I've been feeling the same way sometimes. And I wonder if the answer might not be in those pamphlets?"

"Ah!" I chuckled. "Luis told me all about it. It's quite a story. Full of angels, golden plates. . . it's a little hard to swallow."

"That's what I thought when Angela Fuller first started telling me about it a couple of years ago. But now, I wonder. . . You know, all our lives we've been taught about angels and spirits of good and evil, and saints and sinners. When you stop to think, it's not that much different from what we learned in catechism."

I thought about that. We lay in the dark for a few more minutes, then I abruptly got up and started out of the room. "Where are you going?" Linda wanted to know.

"I'm going to fill the tub with hot water, find those pamphlets and take a good hot soak while I read them."

They *were* interesting.

. . . .

Supper dishes were finally finished and stacked away. Don and Luis were in front of the television set in the day room. On most winter evenings the station was quiet. Kids who flocked over each summer evening to hear Luis read don't come in the winter because we couldn't leave them inside when an alarm hit, and it took too long for them to get their coats on and out the door before we could leave.

I wandered down the hall toward the captain's room. I saw him through the open door, writing the day's events into the station log. I stopped in the doorway.

"C'mon in, Booter," he said without looking up. "I'm almost finished."

I walked in and sat on the chair beside his desk. "D'you remember what time we got off that call to the gas station? I didn't write it down."

I looked at my watch. "About fourteen thirty-five." I'd become so accustomed to twenty-four-hour time I no longer had to stop and figure it out.

"Sounds good," the captain said. His pencil scratched once more, then he stretched back in his chair, hands folded behind his head. "So what's up besides blue sky?"

"Well," I began boldly, "first I'd like you to invite Linda and me to church with you some Sunday. Then I'd like to have a long talk with you."

He laughed, but he didn't look surprised. "Luis told me you've been asking a lot of questions. Sure, you're invited—any Sunday you choose. And afterwards you're invited for dinner. Ellen's great with roast beef!"

I thought I needed to explain, so I said, "I hope Luis will understand. I'd go to his church, but he says he's in one where Spanish is used and I don't speak Spanish."

"He'll understand. Besides, he's in the bishopric out there, so he has his hands full enough on Sunday without visitors." He glanced at the calendar beside his desk. "Let's see, how about this Sunday? Our meetings start at ten."

He closed the log book and set it on the rack. "A long talk, too? Is now a good time?"

I nodded. I was just about to start asking him to tell me about himself and his church when the tones started through the ceiling-mounted speaker. The captain shook his head as he pulled the run card and a pencil from his pocket. "Never fails," he muttered.

"Engine Five. An EMS call, woman badly cut. 2680 South Miranda. 2680 South Miranda. Use channel three."

That wasn't far. Just down the street and around a corner. A small crowd was milling around in the front yard when we pulled up. A thin woman with the sunken eyes of a heroin addict ran up. "She won' open th' door an' she done cut herself all up!" she shouted.

I followed the others up the sidewalk and pushed through the crowd on the dilapidated front porch. Captain Meaker tried the door. "Locked." He peered through the dirty window.

"Can you see her?" cried the small woman.

The captain said, "No."

"She in there. She in there. She be try t' kill herself wid a glass bottle! She bleedin' all over th' place."

The crowd parted and a police woman stepped up to us. She wore corporal's stripes. "What've you got?"

"Attempted suicide, I guess."

"Can you take the door out?"

"Booter, d'you have your tool on your belt?"

I did. The captain had bawled me out once for leaving it behind—and despite his gentle manners Captain David Meaker could deliver a very expert bawling out. Now I slipped it into the lock and twisted. The door popped open.

We stepped inside while the corporal's partner kept the crowd on the porch. Big gouts of blood lay wet on the linoleum floor. I stepped to a door covered by a hanging bedsheet and looked in. "Here she is," I called. She was sprawled in a large chair. Fat. Hugely fat, and covered with smears of crimson.

"Who you?" she asked, bleary eyed.

"Fire department, m'am. We heard you'd hurt yourself."

"I don' need no fire department, or nothin' else fer that matter. You jist leave me 'lone here. I don' need you an' I don' want you here!"

"You're bleeding. . . ."

"Well ain' you jist th' smartes' white boy I ever did see? Sure I bleedin'!"

Captain Meaker and the others crowded into the room. He stepped over and tried to examine one of the large cuts on her shoulders and upper chest. She screamed at him to leave her alone.

Just then, through another door covered with another bedsheet, two boys emerged from the darkness. They stood, wide-eyed, while the woman raved on. "He say I too fat an' I cain't make no more money fer him. He say no man on th' face o' th' earth wanta spend even five bucks on me! So he dump me an' took with some other little slut. . . ."

She swore mightily when the captain tried to touch her.

He looked toward the boys. "Booter," he said, "take those two into the other room."

I herded them past the woman into the kitchen. They sat at the table, wide eyes still peering toward the room we had just left. The big woman still shouted at the captain. I pulled a package of mints from my pocket and offered one to the older boy. He shook his head. The younger one reached up to take it, and I saw his face clearly. It was David, the quiet little boy from the church day care center.

The older boy, about nine or ten, looked up at me. He asked, "Was that Mr. Meaker in there?"

"Yes," I replied. "He's a fireman."

"I know," the boy said. "He comes to our school to help me read and stuff. He's really nice." He paused for a brief moment before he added, "You know something? He really likes me!"

I brushed my hand through the kid's hair. "I think he likes everyone," I answered absently.

David was shivering. I could see that he was wearing nothing more than a T-shirt that was too big for him. I pulled off my turnout coat, sat on a kitchen chair, and wrapped him in my coat. Then I held him on my lap. He was still silent.

The older boy moved closer to me and laid his head on my shoulder. "What's your name?" I asked.

"Mujah," he said. "You spell that m-u-j-a-h. Most white folks don't understand it," he added, matter-of-factly. Then he went on, as if he needed to talk with someone this night. "I'm in the fourth grade. I get mostly A's in school."

The big woman was still shouting and cursing. David curled deeper inside my turnout coat. Mujah's eyes kept snapping back toward the room from which the shouts rolled.

"She gonna die?" he asked.

"No, she's not really badly hurt."

"She does that a lot," the boy said in a whisper. "Someday she's gonna really do it. . . ."

"Is she your mother?"

"Yeah. And she's a doper, too. But she always tells us, 'Don't get inta dope.' She says, 'Look what it's done to me.' She tells me t' do a good job in school and learn everything so I can get outta here someday. She's really nice."

"Where's your father?" I asked, knowing full well what the story probably was.

Mujah just looked at me. "I really like to do math and science. Someday, I'm going to be a scientist and an astronaut. My teacher and Mr. Meaker say I can do it if I try hard enough. . . so I'm trying." He went on, telling me about a project he was doing for a science fair. Something about a collection of animals without backbones. I was only half listening to him and half listening to sounds from the next room. I decided the boy was talking to keep those sounds from his own ears.

I was lost in my thoughts when Captain Meaker, the police woman, and the others came from the room into the kitchen. "Pack it up, Booter. She doesn't want our help."

"But what about these two?" I asked.

The captain shook his head, then he looked at the boy beside me. "Well, hello, Mujah! How are you this evening?"

The boy shrugged. Captain Meaker punched him in the shoulder. In a voice full of forced cheerfulness he said, "Well, hang in there and I'll see you at school tomorrow."

I set David on the floor. The fat woman was still shouting for us to get out of her house. "What about her?"

The police corporal shrugged, "She refuses our help and her injuries aren't life threatening. She doesn't want us here, so we leave."

"Well, what about them?" I indicated the two boys.

"They live here."

"But you can't just leave them. . . ."

"So what do you suggest?"

"Can't you take them into protective custody, or something?"

She shook her head with a wry smile. "Protect them from what? Their mother? I don't see any signs of abuse, do you?"

"But look at her! . . . She's a doper, a whore, . . . suicidal. . . ."

"And their mother! Look, buddy, I'm just a cop. I just enforce the law—I don't write it."

"But. . . ." I couldn't think of any more arguments.

"C'mon, Booter," Captain Meaker prodded me with the first aid box he carried. "Don't make a scene in front of the kids."

I opened my mouth to argue but closed it again when I realized I'd already lost. We left David and Mujah standing alone in the kitchen and walked to the Engine. I was so angry I kept turning around, trying to fight with someone, but I couldn't find anyone to fight except the captain, who kept prodding me with his box, so I exploded on him. "Stop that, dammit!" I shouted. "I'm going. . . I'm going!"

I reached my side of the Engine, whipped my helmet from my head, and threw it as hard as I could into the bucket where my seat was. It ricocheted from the engine cover to the wall and back across toward Luis. He ducked and it missed him by an inch.

"Did that make you feel better?" the captain asked quietly.

I stormed up into my seat, sat down, grabbed the helmet from Luis, buckled my safety belt, and started whispering every swear word I could think of.

That didn't help, either.

. . . .

"Engine Five available," I heard Don's voice in the radio speaker. The captain was busy completing his run card.

"Engine Five, stand by for traffic."

There was a pause and then the tones. "Engine Five, Engine Twenty-two, Ladder Twenty-two, Battalion Three, Utility One. House fire at 2438 South Woodward. 2438 South Woodward. Use channel two."

Don acknowledged and Engine 5 began to roll. I swung around and looked ahead. A large, red glow told me we had a cooker going. I pulled my hood into place, replaced my helmet, and got ready for the battle.

Flames were rolling from most of the windows of an abandoned motel. We were just pulling up to a hydrant and I was ready to jump down when I heard the dispatcher's voice over the radio. It was the first time I'd heard a dispatcher sound excited. "Units responding to 2438 South Woodward," she said. "Be advised police report two small children are inside."

I remembered that abandoned motels often provide housing for transient families, illegal aliens, and all sorts of people who can't afford anything better.

I heard the captain shout something to Don and Engine 5 lurched forward as we passed the hydrant. "Engine Twenty-two, Engine Five." The captain's voice coming back through the speaker was still calm. "Engine Twenty-two, lay in for us, please."

Engine 22 would bring us a hose from the hydrant while we hit the fire faster. I unbuckled my safety belt and grabbed the bar beside me, ready to swing off as soon as we stopped.

Don spotted us in front of the burning building. It was fully engulfed, and I knew anyone inside had little chance of being alive. But you still have to try.

My breathing apparatus slammed down against my back. I was buckling it on the run when I joined Luis and the captain on the way up the sidewalk. Luis had the nozzle as we hit the door of the first motel unit. Flames rolling through the room filled the upper half of the door. We crouched behind the cone of fog spray from the nozzle and duckwalked into the hot room behind it.

Luis swept the nozzle clockwise, following the roll of the flames. The fire was so hot that it re-ignited almost immediately after the spray cone passed. He had to sweep it around several times to blacken even a small amount of fire. As we moved into the room, the fire was lighting up again behind us.

Captain Meaker moved toward the beds and swept his leg under them. Kids try to hide from fires so you search out hiding places. I moved to a closed door and pulled it open. I checked the bathroom. Nothing.

I crawled back into the main room. Luis was crouched in the center sweeping water all around us as the fire still tried to relight. Through his mask speaker the captain shouted, "Back out! There's nobody in here."

We crawled out the door, ready to move to the next unit when a cop met us part way inside. "We got bad information!" he shouted. "They're in the manager's apartment at the other end!"

We all grabbed the hose and began to run, dragging it toward the other end of the long building. Someone grabbed on behind me.

I looked up. It was Felix Mendoza, our friendly neighborhood firebug.

Flame was rolling out the door almost down to floor level. Luis crouched just outside and started water through the door. Flames boiled out and enveloped us for a moment. I ducked my head and turned my face away from heat that penetrated even my heavy clothes. The roll of flame subsided. As we started through the door I caught a glimpse of Engine 22 in the street beside Engine 5.

Progress was slow in the fire's intensity. A lot of water was needed to cool it. We were only part-way into the room when I heard another hose open up beside us. Engine 22 had joined in the fight. Two hoses beat the fire rapidly backwards. We moved through the living room and dropped off into a bedroom while the E22 crew moved up the hall. I was sweeping my leg under the bed when I noticed a small foot under a pile of clothing in the corner beside me.

I jerked the clothing away and shouted that I'd found them. The piled clothing I pulled was still smoldering even though it was wet from our hose. The bigger boy seemed to have been trying to protect the younger one. I grabbed the bigger one and held him under one arm. I was pretty sure he was dead. I grabbed the other and held him under the other arm. Then I stood up as far as I could in the heat and made a run for the front door.

I laid the boys on a couple of turnout coats some men from Ladder 22 had laid out when they saw me coming. I unsnapped my helmet, tossed it into the dirt, pulled my hood down, and yanked the rubber mask from my face. The older boy lay almost naked in the harsh glare of floodlights from Utility 1. His clothing had been burned off and his skin hung in ribbons. Some spots seemed to be charred. I placed my fingers against his throat. Nothing.

The smaller one was still gasping. His chest rose and fell rapidly with the effort. A police officer handed me a dry burn sheet, and I gently covered him. I took an oxygen mask someone offered and fixed it over the little one's face—a burned face. I knew he'd inhaled a lot of heat. His lungs were probably seared.

A man with a paramedic patch on his shoulder shoved me out of his way, so he could move in beside the boy. I knelt in the dirt, watching. A police officer asked if I'd like help taking off my breathing apparatus. Nodding, I unbuckled it. He grabbed the tank and let go with a shout. "Son-of-a-gun! That thing's hot!"

Paramedics wrapped the little one and laid him on a gurney. A cop covered the bigger one. I got up and walked to the motel's black shell to help with the overhaul.

Later, fire investigators told us that someone had pitched milk jugs full of gasoline into each unit of the long motel and lit the match. "Probably didn't know anyone was inside," one investigator said.

I told him I'd seen Felix there. "I know, we saw him too. And, believe me, we're going to have a long, long talk with him."

. . . .

Don backed the Engine into the house. I headed first for the pop machine, then for the shower. I was standing in the hot stream of water drinking orange soda when the tones hit again. I leaped into my sweaty pants and boots and bunker pants, waiting just outside the shower stall, and followed the others to the Engine.

I did that twice more before I finished my shower. We ran on two auto accidents and a false alarm. I didn't think I'd sleep that night, but I did.

After I got home in the morning, I called the hospital. At first the duty nurse in the emergency room didn't want to give out any information, but when I told her I'd pulled the little guy out, she said, "Oh. . . well, I'm sorry, but he passed away around midnight."

I called my brother-in-law, told him I wouldn't be in to work that day, and went out and ran about six miles.

Chapter Eighteen

We met Captain Meaker and his family outside the church before ten o'clock that next Sunday morning. Linda had been excited when I'd told her about going. She'd been up and ready to go before I'd even opened my eyes.

We walked into the church's hallway and were greeted by a dozen people before we'd taken a dozen steps. Every one of the men shook my hand, and so did some of the women. I noticed right off that the Meakers were the only Black people there, yet the captain and his family seemed to fit right in. Judging by the way others greeted and talked with them, they were well liked and respected.

"We have three meetings back to back in a three hour time period," Ellen Meaker told us. "There's Priesthood for the men and boys, Primary for the little ones, Relief Society for the women—then Sunday school and, finally, Sacrament meeting."

Captain Meaker took me aside. "Since I don't hold the Priesthood, I don't attend Priesthood meetings. Instead, I teach a Primary class. But I'll introduce you to the Elder's quorum president, and you can go to the Priesthood meeting with him."

I shook my head. "I'll stick with you." Then I added, "After all, I'm not a priest either."

He smiled and motioned for me to follow him. I spent the next hour helping him try to keep a wiggling bunch of eight-year-old boys corralled long enough to teach them about someone named Nephi. Then I followed him back down the hall where we met Ellen and Linda for Sunday school.

The lesson that day was way over my head. In all my years at St. Stephanie's I'd never heard such depth in any discussion. I suddenly realized that, in this church, I might have a chance of finally answering questions that had rattled around my brain since eighth grade. In the hall after Sunday school there was more hand shaking as we moved toward what they called the "chapel."

I crossed myself from habit as I entered the chapel. Then I looked around sheepishly to see if anyone had noticed. The captain had, and he winked at me. I smiled and followed him in, thankful that I hadn't genuflected, too. Inside, the chapel was absolutely plain. No statues. No stained glass windows. No crucifix above the altar. In fact, I couldn't even find an altar. There was a pulpit—but no altar.

A few people walked up to sit on the raised stage at the front of the chapel. We sat in about the fourth row. With the Meaker family, we pretty well filled a whole row. The chapel was smaller than any church I'd ever been in. It seemed cramped—especially since it didn't have outside windows.

A woman began to play the organ. I figured the processional would start any minute. But when she stopped playing a man stood up and began to make announcements. I heard Ellen whisper to Linda, "He's the bishop."

Bishop? I thought. He's not wearing robes.

I kept waiting for the processional, for altar boys, for someone who looked *official,* but I saw only three men, in business suits, sitting behind the pulpit. I leaned over to ask the captain, "Which one is the priest?"

He looked puzzled, then he smiled. "They're all priests. The one speaking is the Bishop. I guess he's sort of chief priest. The other two are his counselors. Assistant priests, if you want to call them that."

We sang a hymn—sitting down. Then a young woman walked forward and offered a simple prayer which sounded similar to those I'd been hearing every third morning for seven months. Next, two boys who couldn't have been more than sixteen or seventeen knelt and prayed over bread and water—the only people I saw kneeling all that day. The bread and water was served to all of us by little boys. "Deacons," Captain Meaker called them.

After the deacons finished, one of them went to the pulpit and gave a short talk which I had trouble understanding. The kid was obviously scared to death, and he spoke in a whisper that even the microphone couldn't pick up. As he walked away from the pulpit, with a look of pure relief on his face, one of the counselors grabbed his arm, pulled him down onto the seat beside him, grabbed him in a head lock, tussled up his hair, turned him loose, and gave him a swat on the fanny to send him on his way. I grinned inwardly, thinking what a stir something like that would cause in a Mass.

Two men followed the boy. "High councilors," Captain Meaker explained. I nodded even though I had no idea what a high councilor might be. One of them talked about how he believed the story of Joseph Smith and his golden plates to be really true—and I wondered why he should have to tell people that if they all believed it. The other man spoke of what he called "temple marriage" and told us how we could go on in eternity, together, instead of separating at death. That brought to mind words the priest had spoken when Linda and I had stood before the altar. ". . . and until death shall you part. . . ." I sat up and took notice. This was a new idea that excited me, somehow.

Another hymn, also sung sitting down—and a prayer by an old man who didn't seem to know how much was enough—ended the meeting. We filed out to the parking lot. It took a long time to get out of there. It seemed the Meakers had a lot of visiting to do and everyone they met wanted them to introduce us.

At the Meaker's home, Ellen and Linda disappeared into the kitchen while the captain, his boys, and I wandered down to the family room. They pulled board games from a closet and I began to play checkers with Kenneth. It was hard to keep my mind on the game—a mind filled with questions that wanted to be asked. So, while I tried to play checkers, I asked the captain some of them. Listening to his answers gave Kenneth the advantage. He whipped me twice.

We ate, then we sat in the living room. The rest of the afternoon, Linda and I had a lot of questions and Ellen and the captain had a lot of answers. There was one question I wanted to ask in the worst way, but I hesitated. Finally, I managed to get it out. "Could I ask you something that may be too personal?"

"Shoot," he nodded.

"Well," I stammered, "if you can't be a full member of this church, why do you belong to it?"

He was quiet for a few seconds. Then he said, slowly, "Well... to tell the truth, I wonder that myself, sometimes. It's a pretty long story."

Bryan was asleep on his lap, and he paused while Ellen laid the boy on the floor. Then the captain took a deep breath and told us how it had been to grow up in the South Valley when kids his color had to sit in the back of the bus, when restrooms were marked "Colored" and "White."

"I had a lot of bitterness built up inside me by the time I got out of high school," the captain said.

He'd joined the Navy and stumbled into medical corpsman training. Martin Luther King was marching in Alabama when Dave Meaker shipped out for Vietnam. He told of the loneliness there; of the bodies they brought back, in bags, aboard the gunship helicopters; of his first combat missions with Marine units.

He told us of the fear he had felt and how he'd gone looking for something to give comfort. Then he told of how he'd gone into DaNang one night intent on becoming roaring drunk and how he had met another corpsman there—a white man. They'd hit it off somehow, and he'd joined the other guy in drinking Coke instead of the powerful rice whiskey he'd intended to buy.

The story of a growing friendship continued. The buddy was a Mormon and he'd filled the captain's head with his strange ideas. Then came a day when Captain Meaker and his Marine unit were set down smack in the middle of a Viet Cong Battalion. Before the day was over, most of them were dead. The captain, badly wounded himself, was holding the enemy from the other wounded men. He held them at bay, with an automatic rifle, until rescue helicopters and gunships arrived.

They'd flown the captain home. Pinned a second purple heart on him, gave him the Congressional Medal of Honor and made him a Navy recruiter for the rest of his hitch. After he got out, he'd joined a private ambulance company as one of the first paramedics in the state. Then he signed on with the fire department as soon as they'd opened recruiting for Blacks.

And the buddy in Vietnam? Captain Meaker shook his head. "I don't know. I never heard from him or of him. But his ideas stuck in my head. One day, for some reason I don't fully understand, I picked up the phone and called a number I'd seen in the phone book. 'Mormon missionaries,' it said."

We talked some more, had dessert, and left—long after darkness had fallen.

I sat in the living room while Linda showered. While I sat there, I picked up the phone book. I looked under "M". Sure enough, there it was: "Mormon missionaries."

Chapter Nineteen

I didn't dial that number, and I didn't tell Linda about it. I guess I still wasn't quite ready for such a step. I felt caught in the middle of a squeeze play. My mother called every Saturday asking us to attend Mass with her, and she had talked my father back into treatment for his drinking. I couldn't mention anything to them about the Mormon church. Mom had enough on her mind, and my father's progress in his rehabilitation program was tenuous, at best. I figured that if I so much as mentioned the word "Mormon," it would set him off again and shatter her dreams for him.

My mind was in almost constant turmoil those days. Linda wanted to attend church with the Meakers every week, but I was afraid my father would find out. I welcomed the weeks when A-shift pulled Sunday duty.

Sunday in a firehouse is generally quiet. Except for the routine duties of checking and maintaining equipment, and cleaning the house, there isn't much to do except wait for the tones.

Sunday duty had really disturbed me at first because I had felt so out of place in the routine Don, Luis, and the captain had established for themselves. But through the months I'd been working Station 5 I had come to look forward to Sunday. Now, with such an upheaval in my life, Sundays at the station had become days of respite.

We started each Sunday, like all days in Station 5, with a prayer. Then we worked like mad to get station chores finished in time to switch on the television, so we could watch the Mormon Tabernacle Choir's weekly broadcast. And, while in the beginning of my time there, I used to find something to do in the hose tower or someplace else far from the television, I had become the one who turned the set on and called the others to watch. I noticed, too, the great contrast between the quiet dignity of the choir and the spoken word and the loud, Bible-thumping exhortations of Sunday preachers on other channels. I also noticed how often speakers on the other channels begged for money and made special offers of trinkets or prayers in return for donations. It reminded me of dropping money in the box every time you lit a candle or said a prayer at one of the side altars in St. Stephanie's.

Don did have a good voice, as I'd suspected from the first, and he made no bones about his ambition to sing with the Tabernacle Choir some day. I have a good voice, too, and often he and I would sing along with the choir—much to the amusement, I think, of Luis and the captain.

After the choir broadcast, an hour was reserved for what the others called "scripture reading." They would find quiet spots and curl up with books or magazines. They'd often interrupt their reading to ask each other questions or to discuss something they'd read.

I'd made myself very scarce during those hours in the first couple of months I'd been in Station 5. The Engine was a little shinier then. But, gradually, I'd come to picking up the magazines where they had been left lying and started sneaking a little reading in the privacy of places like the potty booth.

By February, I'd stopped trying to hide my reading activities. The magazines had led me to curiosity about the "Golden Bible" the Protestant preacher had railed against in his book, *The Mormon Church Exposed*. I remember the first time I sneaked a peek at the "Golden Bible." Don had been sitting at the kitchen table, books piled beside him, while he worked on a talk for the next Sunday's church meeting. When he left for a few minutes, I picked up his Book of Mormon and began thumbing through it.

My eye caught a story about an iron rod, a big building full of mocking people, a foul river—and before I knew what was happening to me, I was sitting in a chair in the bunk room, reading more while Don was turning the station upside down, looking for his book.

The week after Linda and I went to church with the captain and his family, Don offered me a paperbound copy of my own Book of Mormon.

Occasionally on a Sunday afternoon, some of the families would wander by the station. Linda started coming by with Ellen Meaker, and I could tell that the two were becoming good friends. Sometimes the captain would get his guitar and we'd spend time singing together. There was a warmth there that attracted me.

Maybe it was because there hadn't been much warmth in a house with an alcoholic father.

. . . .

But Sundays at Station 5 weren't completely idyllic. We still ran to fires, false alarms, auto accidents, and an occasional Sunday school meeting of the knife-and-gun-society. It was on a Sunday that I got hurt on the job for the first time. Looking back, I know that accident helped change my life and the lives of a couple of others, too.

We had just finished supper. Don's family left and I was putting dishes in cupboards when the tones hit. "Engine Five, Engine Sixteen, Engine Twenty-two, Ladder Twenty-two, Ladder Four, Battalion Three, Utility One. Structure fire at the Commonwealth Hotel, 1380 West Van Horne. Commonwealth Hotel, 1380 West Van Horne. Use channel One."

We'd been to the Commonwealth Hotel before. It was one of a dozen large, abandoned buildings in our area. All the buildings were ready to collapse. All had violations of the building code that demands destruction of any buildings in such unsafe condition. But, despite collapsed stairways, sagging floors, and cracked walls, the owners packed enough clout in city politics that they didn't have to worry about the expense of getting rid of the buildings. Old hotels, factories, apartment houses simply sat baking in the sun and freezing up again in winter while rats, mice, and transient humans took shelter in them.

Winter fires in the buildings were generally the result of warming fires built by transients. And when, from time to time, an owner did decide to demolish one it was usually done by a torch—a paid arsonist.

That night was unusually cold and Captain Meaker hit it right when he remarked on the way to the engine bay, "Looks like the Commonwealth residents got cold."

We rolled up, hooked a hydrant, and laid in. Smoke was showing from the east side of the second floor. I had trouble loosening one of the hydrant caps. When I finally caught up with the captain and Luis they were starting to crawl down the debris-filled second floor hallway.

The smoke was heavy and oily. Even with the light clipped to the rim of my helmet, it was impossible to see more than a few inches, but we did see a dim glow of flames licking from a door at the end of the hall. I dropped back to help the hose couplings slide around the corner at the top of the stairs. When I heard the nozzle open, I pulled up a little slack hose and began crawling down the hall to join the others at the fire.

I was about halfway down the hall when I felt a sudden sharp pain in the palm of my right hand—where the thumb joins the wrist. I tried to jerk it away from whatever was causing the pain, but it seemed to be stuck. The more I tried to pull, the more it hurt. I tried calling for help even though I knew there was no way they could hear me over the nozzle noise.

Crouching down, I was able to bring the beam of my helmet light onto my hand. The sight made my stomach churn. I'd put my hand down squarely on a large nail—about a 16-penny. It had penetrated completely through my hand and was protruding through the glove at the bottom of my wrist. I began to get nauseated, so I looked away. Throwing up in a smoke mask isn't fun.

Gradually, I brought my stomach under control. I took a quick inventory of the situation and decided I was in no danger. The smoke was lifting as water did its work on the fire. I could wait for help. The nozzle was still working ahead of me when I heard someone come up behind me. I swung my headlamp beam around and saw a helmet with L22 reflecting from its side. They started to crawl past, ready to begin a victim search in the rooms along the hall.

"Hey, guys," I called out, amazed at how calm I was. "Hold up a minute, will you? I have a little problem here."

They stopped. "What's up?"

"Got a nail up through my hand."

The closest one crouched so his light lit my hand. "Ouch!" he said. "Looks nasty!"

The Ladder captain crawled up. "What's this? Some sort of convention?"

"E Five's Booter has a nail through his hand. He's stuck."

"Lemme see." The captain crouched, looked, and then said, "Son of a gun!"

"Can we pull him loose?" their booter asked.

"No, better get the K-12."

The ladder's boot, a kid named Parker Jones, left to get the power saw while the others examined the situation. Someone had dropped a full sheet of 3/4 inch plywood on the floor with one big nail sticking up through it.

"Bat Three. Ladder Twenty-two captain," the captain spoke into his radio. "We have E Five's boot injured up here. Injuries are minor—he has a nail through his hand. Send another crew to search floor two."

His radio crackled and I recognized Captain Meaker's voice. "Ladder Twenty-two captain. Engine Five captain. Did you say our boot is hurt?"

"Ten-four."

"I wondered where he was. Can you send a man to help with the nozzle? We've almost got it licked, and I'd like to come back down there." A moment later I saw his light bobbing down the hall as he crawled toward us.

He took a quick look. "Why'd you go and do that?" he asked.

The Bat Chief himself came up with the K-12 power saw. They cut the plywood away as close to my hand as they could and walked me down the stairs with a square piece of plywood firmly attached to my hand.

A paramedic examined me while his partner kept repeating, "Why don't we do a field amputation? I've never done a field amputation." Firefighters don't get much mercy from other firefighters. It's not part of the code of ethics.

It was a quick ambulance ride to the hospital. One thing about being a firefighter—emergency room people figure you're one of the family. They give our injuries first priority. It wasn't long before a doctor was clucking around me. I sat up on the examining table. "Do you want to lie down while I work?" he asked.

"Nah, I'm okay," I replied.

"Suit yourself," he answered as he drove a needle of Xylocaine into the hole beside the nail. They told me later that I got the concussion when I fainted and fell off the table.

. . . .

The bandage on my right hand was huge. With the swelling my hand was huge, too. "How long will you be off?" Captain Meaker asked when he telephoned the next morning.

"At least four weeks," I replied.

"Some people have all the luck," he laughed. "What will you do with your vacation? Hawaii? Acapulco? The Riviera?"

"Porter's Body and Paint Shop. I'm going to earn some extra money."

"Don't forget, I'm your captain. I get ten percent."

"I thought you Mormons say that only God gets ten percent."

His voice turned harsh. "Booter," he reminded me, "Don't you *ever* forget that in Station Five, I *am* God!"

We laughed and hung up.

But I didn't earn much money. There wasn't a thing I could do around the body shop with my hand in that enormous bandage.

I was bored silly by Wednesday. Linda had a student teaching seminar at the university that night, so I drove down to Station 5 for supper. They were out when I got there, but supper was cooling in the oven. I turned the oven back on and washed and baked some potatoes and had a regular feast ready when they came back.

Don saw me first. "Some people don't have *any* sense," he muttered. "Vacation time—and what do you do? Y'hang around here, of all places!"

"I guess I'm bored."

Some hose had gotten muddy, so supper waited while we laid a new shift of inch-and-a-half up in the forward Mattydale. I helped with my left hand. "Bored, huh?" the captain asked. "How'd you like to meet some really good people and help them at the same time?" He invited me to come to the school at the end of the street next morning. "There's a lot to do there. They need all the help they can get."

I wasn't too sure about the idea of trying to help little kids, but I decided to give it a try.

. . . .

Captain Meaker's truck was already in the school's parking lot when I pulled in at eight the next morning. He led me inside and introduced me to some of the teachers and the principal, who was a very businesslike Black woman. She led me to a room halfway down the hall and told me how to help the kids with reading. She explained that many of the children spoke little English when they entered the school. Others came from families in which both parents were unable to read or write much more than their names.

A bell rang and a herd of kids came trooping down the halls. Captain Meaker set up a pile of books on another table in the room. "Get ready," he said, "because here they come—ready or not!"

One of the first ones through the door was Mujah. He headed straight for the captain's table, then stopped short when he caught sight of me. He broke into a huge grin. "Hi, Mister Boot, are you going to help Mr. Meaker?"

I looked at him. "Who told you my name was Mr. Boot?"

"He did," Mujah replied, pointing to the grinning captain.

I shook my head and answered, "Yes. At least I'm going to try."

"Good!" Mujah exclaimed. Then he turned to other kids who were pouring through the door. "Hey! This is Mr. Boot; he's a fireman, and he's my friend!" Then, turning back to me he said with finality, "You can work with me."

"How's your mother, Mujah?" I asked, trying to seem friendly.

Mujah just looked at me and said nothing. "That's a question you don't ask here," the principal whispered.

What I learned in the next few minutes scared and appalled me. Mujah, bright as he seemed to be, could barely read. Angela, a little Mexican girl with beautiful brown eyes and a very dirty face above a very dirty dress, couldn't even begin to figure out the simplest words. The other four at the table were no better.

The principal sat beside me. "What's wrong with them?" I whispered. "They don't seem to be retarded or anything."

She shook her head grimly. "Ask some of them how many times they've changed schools."

Mujah counted on his fingers. "Six, I think," he answered.

"He's in fourth grade," the principal whispered. "Can you imagine what a little stability would do for his life?"

We struggled through, trying to unravel the mysterious sounds of letters, until a bell rang. The kids began to clatter from the room, but Mujah stopped suddenly beside my chair, grabbed my shirt, and leaned down close to my ear. "Mr. Boot," he said, "I really *like* you. . . ." Then he dashed off down the hall.

The principal was getting ready for the next group. "Mujah told me, the night I first met him, that he makes all A's in school. How can he do that when he can't read?" I asked.

She smiled and shook her head. "He has a big imagination. He does make high marks in anything he can learn without reading. He's a whiz in math and science. But, otherwise. . .all he can do is dream."

I understood.

That night was spent making little cards with letters and animals all over them. I spent every day at the school until my hand healed. I'm not sure how much I taught them, but I know that Angela, Paul, Ramon, Mujah and the others taught me a lot more than I taught them.

And in the evenings, when Linda came home from her school and I came home from mine, we'd share stories of little funnies, of successes and frustrations. And when Linda remarked once, "You sure can become attached to those little people," I understood exactly what she meant.

Chapter Twenty

It was the end of March before the Department doctor signed certification that I was fit for duty again. Dad had fallen off the wagon and was drinking heavier than before, and Linda and I had a heated discussion about it. She'd argued that we couldn't put our entire lives on hold waiting for him to get his head pulled together. "You can't go on using him as an excuse for not looking deeper into the Church," she said. Her dark eyes brimmed with tears.

I finally agreed and we called Ellen Meaker to ask what we should do next.

"Come over for dinner tonight, and we'll talk about it," she answered.

We did, and as we drove into their driveway, I spotted two bicycles parked under the carport. Somehow, I knew whose bicycles they were.

The missionaries were nice kids. One was from Utah someplace, and the other was from Florida. My first impression was that they could eat more than anyone I'd ever met outside a firehouse. But then I decided that bicycles need fuel, too.

We spent the next three free evenings at Meaker's listening to the missionaries' "discussions." They told us about a boy named Joseph Smith who had gone to a grove of trees to pray. He had prayed for guidance in deciding which of a number of churches he should join. I understood exactly how he must have felt.

We learned that Mormons believe they have a prophet who leads their church. As Catholics believe the Pope has a direct line to God, so the Mormons believe their President has one, too. But they go a step further—they believe their President has the *only* direct line.

I think the most impressive thing they taught was the idea that the Mormon church was the true church—restored after the original church had fallen away from Christ's original teachings. That idea explained a question I'd had for years. Ever since junior high school, when St. Stephanie's nuns and brothers had told me about Martin Luther King and other Protestant reformers, I'd wondered what things in the church had needed reforming—our teachers had tried hard not to be very specific. It suddenly became clear when one of the missionaries began talking about what he called "the principle of repentance." He mentioned the old church's practice of selling indulgences—grants of forgiveness.

That hit me right between the eyes. It was the core of one of the things that bothered me most about my church. I'd been upset for a long time with the idea that a person could go out any night of the week, do whatever he pleased, visit the Confessional on Saturday, say a few *Hail Mary's* or *Our Fathers,* drop an offering in the poor box and be ready to go do it again next week with a clear conscience.

That didn't sit square with what I thought I had read in the Bible.

Another thing that I found attractive was the sense of family the Mormons seemed to have. The strong emphasis on family activities and family strength really appealed to me—maybe because it was something I felt had been lacking from my own life.

We learned other things, too. Tithing, Priesthood, Eternal Marriage.

Eternal Marriage—now that was one that *really* grabbed me. I looked at Linda and realized how much I loved her. Maybe it was because I saw death so often on the job and had come to understand how thin the line is between life and death—whatever it was, I saw that principle as a chance for great happiness and comfort.

The Word of Wisdom was another idea that appealed to me. It teaches abstinence from drinking and smoking. I realized that I'd almost stopped using coffee. It wasn't available in the station—and I'd never felt good about brewing any just for me—and I had soon found out I felt better without it. As for drinking, I'd stopped completely after that day I'd gone to Captain Meaker's house.

So much of what they said made such good sense that it overcame the strangeness of some of the ideas they presented. Finally, one of them popped the question I'd been anticipating and dreading at the same time. "Well," he asked, "could we challenge you to accept baptism?"

Linda said, "Yes," with no hesitation. But I held off. I still wasn't sure, and I asked for some to think about it.

We shook hands with everyone and drove home in silence until we reached the apartment parking lot. "What's wrong?" Linda asked.

I shook my head. "I don't know," I answered. "I don't know. In one way, I believe all of it. But in another, I'm just not sure." I sighed. "I just don't know," I said again.

She said she understood. We left it at that.

The next Sunday was the first Sunday in April and A-shift was on duty. We finished our chores, and about 9 o'clock the families came in and soon were settled in front of the television. Don told me that the church holds general conferences twice a year. Conference is a time when the church's leaders can speak directly to the people. Linda had come in with Ellen and the kids, so we curled up in a big chair to watch together.

The whole conference broadcast was dignified, quiet, and full of plain common sense. I listened carefully, even though there were parts of it that went right over my head. Like when a little old man they all called Brother Richards spoke of something from the scriptures. But, generally, I understood it all, and it all seemed to make good sense.

The younger kids had become restless and had gone into the bunkroom to play ping pong or rattle the weight lifting machine. The final speaker was a small man who spoke with a raspy voice. Don's son spoke up. "I'm named for him," Kimball Spencer remarked.

The man, who was president of the Church, spoke quietly and firmly, and we all listened carefully. He was about halfway through his talk when a tremendous crash echoed from the bunk room, and little Bryan began crying. Captain Meaker got up and headed through the locker room to see what was happening. While he was gone, Ellen leaned over and whispered, "Dave just loves this man. He has the idea that it will be President Kimball who will finally grant the Priesthood to our people. But I worry some. He's looking older every time we see him."

The captain came back with Bryan, wrapping the boy's fingers in a wet washrag. "Caught it in the weights," he explained.

It was a little hard to hear the television over Bryan's muffled sobs, but I did hear Spencer W. Kimball say one thing that stuck with me after the broadcast was over. He said, ". . . and let him who seeks the truth seek the answers through prayer—through fervent, earnest prayer."

. . . .

We ate a meal, from casseroles the women had brought, and settled down for the afternoon session of conference. Those words about prayer kept running through my head and I was looking forward to hearing more.

But I didn't. The first speaker was just being introduced when we were called out. A child who'd broken an arm in a fall down some stairs in the highrise ghetto needed our attention. Don had just backed into the engine bay when the tones hit again. Someone had tried to drive away from a gas pump up on Van Horne without taking the hose from the tank's opening. It burned up half the gas station.

The conference was over by the time we got back.

. . . .

Just before shift change the next morning, the phone rang. Chief Halvorsen asked if I would double back for a shift in Engine 4. "That's quite an honor," Don remarked, running his fingers through his thinning hair. "Department usually frowns on Boots doubling with unfamiliar companies." He punched me a friendly punch. "But you're gaining a pretty good name for yourself, you know that?"

That made me feel good.

Station 4 is just the other side of the downtown business district. The station houses an Engine and a Ladder and sits tucked between a MacDonalds on one side and a Methodist church on the other. It's an older, two story station with real fire poles from the upstairs bunk room to the engine bay below. That tickled me because I'd never slid down a fire pole.

I mentioned that to Tom Fuller, captain of Engine 4. He laughed. "Well, don't you get any ideas about having to run upstairs to slide down the pole when the alarm hits." Then he thought about it for a second before he added, "Tell you what—you clean up the bunk room this morning. Then you can slide down the pole."

I cleaned the bunk room, hoping all the while to hear the tones for Engine 4, but nothing happened. Finally, when I'd finished cleaning around the bunks, I slid down the pole just for the heck of it. I landed with a crash in a big heap. Those things are slippery! Thank goodness everyone else was in the kitchen or dayroom, and no one saw my arrival on the floor.

We had no runs during the day. We pulled a dozen building inspections but went no place fast. There seems to be an axiom in the fire service that says, "Want a run? Then climb into the shower, sit down to dinner, get comfortable on the potty. . . . You'll get a run!"

I set my bunker pants tucked around my boots and climbed into the shower after a hard fitness workout that afternoon. Sure enough, I'd just worked up a good lather when the tones hit. I tried to rinse a little of the soap off before I bailed out, pulled my uniform pants over my wet legs, and jumped into my boots. I jerked the bunkers up, hauled the suspenders over my shoulders, and headed down the hall, pulling a T-shirt over the suspenders. Anything you can get on under the turnout gear is just more protection from heat.

I hadn't heard the dispatch because I'd been trying to rinse when it was broadcast. "Where're we going?" I asked Manuel Rodriguez who sat across the engine cover from me.

"We got one on the sixteenth floor of the Trust Bank Building," he answered. "We're the first-due Engine."

I took a deep breath. Highrise fires are the stuff nightmares are made of. Some of the towering buildings were built with fire safety in mind, but until the Federal government got involved, and Congress passed some highrise safety laws, the laws of dollars and cents prevailed. Even so, Congress, in its eternal wisdom, exempted Federal highrises from the laws. I guess they thought fires burn differently when they're Federally owned.

A Battalion Chief reached the Trust Building before we did. He was barking instructions over the radio as fast as he could. He'd already called second and third alarms, so I knew we had something interesting happening.

We laid doubles off a hydrant whose green cap told us it was fed by a large water main. Then we gathered at the lobby door and waited. I'd been looking up but all I could see was a few wisps of smoke against the evening sky—'way up in the sky. I couldn't see the need for the second and third alarms and figured the chief was just playing it safe. But then I noticed the large number of people who were streaming out of the lobby and I understood. He was worried about rescue.

I was surprised. Highrise firefighting is a whole different ballgame. We didn't go rushing into the lobby. Instead, we stood there until a rather large group of men were assembled. Then we all handed the chief's aide our tracking tags—metal tags with our names on them—so he could keep track of who was in the building and who had left it. (We have other metal tags riveted to our coats so they can identify our bodies if they need to.)

Finally the Bat 5 Chief began leading us up the stairs. We travelled light. We'd use hoses from hose boxes located on each floor's stair landings. Sixteen flights. The elevators in the Trust Bank Building lacked the capability for fire department control—it wasn't required when the place was built, and installing it now would cost more than two or three Engine companies. Elevators have a way of running to the fire floor and opening their doors. In fact, just a few days earlier, I'd seen a clip on the news about five firefighters in some Eastern city who'd ridden the elevator up. It hit the fire floor, stopped, and opened its door on a furnace. I guess their department had to use the little metal tags on their coats when they found their bodies.

So we hiked upwards. By the tenth floor, we were all blowing pretty hard. We hit smoke at the twelfth floor so we took a break, got our breathing under control, and pulled on our masks. There was no heat until we reached the sixteenth floor landing. There it was hotter than a gun barrel. Paint, on the outside of the metal fire door that closed the stairwell, was blistering and smoking.

The Bat Chief motioned us down the stairs. We crossed the fifteenth floor to another stairwell and moved back up to floor 16 again. The chief unlocked a cabinet in the stair-landing wall and we pulled two two-and-a-half-inch hoses from the locker. I grabbed the nozzle of one, and two men backed me up. Someone turned water into the hoses; I flushed air and signalled the chief that I was ready. He nodded to a Ladder man who popped the door with his Halligan tool.

Both of us on the nozzles opened up as soon as the door popped, but there was no fire on the other side. We shut down and began to walk warily down the hall. Another metal door halfway down the hall stopped us. It was blistered and paint on the wall surrounding it was beginning to discolor.

"Down!" the chief ordered. We crouched as low as we could get. My heart was pounding as the Ladder man set his Halligan. We opened up on the closed door and steam rolled from it as the truckie jerked sideways on the tool's handle. The door popped and we were looking into the mouth of a blast furnace. It must have been a heck of an experience for those guys back east when that elevator door opened!

We shoved the fire down the hall, pausing at each open door to snuff the flames in side rooms. We reached the other end of the hall just as the first of our bells began ringing. Another crew moved in behind and relieved us while we went back down to the fifteenth floor landing and changed air bottles. Some poor souls had packed those bottles all the way up there.

We rested. Another crew was operating two floors above us checking the seventeenth floor for fire and victims. Radios don't work very well inside metal and concrete buildings, so the chief was talking on a telephone that was located inside the hose box. "Check the sprinkler valves," he was saying. "None of the sprinklers were operating up here." I figured someone had closed a valve someplace.

Bells began ringing above us so we moved back up to floor 16 and down the hall to where our relief crew was still pulling ceiling and wall panels, chasing down the last of the lingering hot spots. The occupancy had been the mail room of a large insurance company. Paper and printing fluids had fed the fire.

We'd been lucky, though. Even though the sprinklers which could have snuffed the fire when it was a baby didn't work, the automatic fire doors had worked.

It was midnight before we left. I was glad to get some sack time that night!

Chapter Twenty-One

I missed the kids at the school, so I worked out a compromise with my brother-in-law. I worked a little later each evening and spent the mornings of my days off at the school. Progress with those kids was frustratingly slow, but there *was* some progress—and that, I guess, was what kept me going back. That, and something else that was awfully hard to define.

Linda kept after me to call the missionaries back and make arrangements for joining the church. But Mom still called us nearly every Saturday and asked us to Mass. Then, one Saturday, I answered the phone in the day room at the station. Mom hadn't found Linda at home, so she'd called me there.

I stuttered around, trying to find a way to tell her no without hurting her feelings. Finally I blurted, "Mom. . . listen, will you? I just don't feel comfortable at Mass any more."

"Why?" she asked simply.

I tried to evade the answer. "I just don't," I replied. "It just doesn't seem right anymore."

There was a long pause. Then she asked quietly, "You've been going to the Mormon Church, haven't you?"

I looked up at the ceiling for a long moment, trying to think of a good answer. I finally decided the truth was best, so I said, "Yes."

After a pause she said, "Oh, dear. I hope you know what you're doing. Your father will be furious."

I nodded even though I knew she couldn't see me. "Yes, I suppose he will."

"You won't go to Mass, then?" She was still trying.

"No, Mother. Not for now, at least."

She was silent again. Then, "Well, son, it *is* your life." She paused then she added, "But I love you. And God bless you, no matter what you decide."

Then she hung up abruptly.

I stood there holding the telephone handset. Captain Meaker looked up from reading the newspaper. He was frowning. "Trouble?"

"No. Well, yeah. I guess so. . . ."

I walked to the apparatus bay and began rearranging my gear on the floor and on the Engine. The captain followed me. "I hope you won't think I'm being nosy or something. But if you need to talk, I'm here." Then he walked out to the front lawn where he began pulling spring weeds from between tulips and daffodils that were just beginning to die with late spring.

I stood there thinking. Finally I followed him outside. Luis was sitting in the warm evening air. A few kids gathered around while he read to them. Don was repainting the barbeque grill beside the kitchen door. "Cap," I started, "I just can't seem to make up my mind. . . ."

"About what?"

"About the church. I've read, I've listened to the missionaries, I've listened to the conference. It all makes sense—good sense. But somehow it's still scrambled up." I kicked some dirt off the cement. "I guess my head tells me it's right, but my heart still isn't sure."

He nodded. "Yeah, I know what you mean."

"You do?"

"Sure. I think all of us who join the Church go through that. Heck, I still do, sometimes. Here I am—can't hold the Priesthood—half the blessings of the Church are out of my reach. Do you think I don't wonder about it sometimes?"

I bent down and plucked a dandelion from the grass. "President Kimball says we can pray to find out, and I've tried. But, do you know what? I don't really know how to pray! All I know is the Our Father and how to say the Hail Mary. And the Lord's prayer just doesn't seem appropriate right now."

He nodded understanding. "Prayers have to come from the heart."

"So how do you do it?"

"Well, there's the correct order of prayer. First you call upon our Heavenly father. Then you can offer thanks for what you have, then you ask for the blessings you need. Finally, you simply close in the name of Jesus Christ. It's quite simple. We follow the same pattern in our morning prayers." He shrugged. "It seems to work."

"So, if I pray about it like the missionaries said I should, I'll find out what's right?"

"Yep."

I pulled more dandelions.

"So how will I know?"

"You'll know."

That didn't help much and I said so.

"I can't explain any better. . . you'll just *know!* The book says there'll be a 'burning in your bosom.' You'll know. . . ."

Don had come around the corner. He'd been listening. "You know the best place I've found for praying? In the mountains. I go find me a little trout stream. . . ."

Captain Meaker laughed. "I suppose you're going to tell us that God is a fly fisherman?"

Don smiled. "He must be. Only a fly fisherman would have included trout streams in his world. But, seriously, there's something about the peace and quiet—running water—mountains. . . ."

I laughed, too. "Don's right, Cap. Didn't Moses and Jesus himself do their praying on mountaintops?"

"Yeah," the captain acknowledged. "But I don't remember reading about trout streams."

"Well," Don suggested, "I have an idea. We're all off next Saturday. What say we go up to the mountains and try it? We can leave the women at home, take the boys, and go help the Boot commune with nature and God."

"Sounds good to me," I said.

It was decided.

. . . .

That Sunday I read everything I could find about prayer. When we went back to work on Tuesday, I decided to try it. When Don called us to the dayroom for prayer, I was ready.

"Whose turn is it?" asked Captain Meaker.

"Mine!" I said firmly.

They all looked surprised. They'd never asked me to pray, and I'd never volunteered. We knelt and I began. It was simple, and it left me with a good feeling. I decided I'd read all I could that week; and when Saturday came, I'd find time to get off by myself. Maybe I'd even find a grove of trees to pray in. That idea excited me, somehow.

. . . .

I didn't tell Linda about my plan. That was too personal to talk about, even with her. I could tell that Mom hadn't said anything to my father about our phone conversation the week before because I hadn't heard any explosions from that part of town.

On Wednesday, while I was listening to Mujah struggle through his reading, a thought suddenly struck me; and when the bell rang, I asked him to wait a moment. I didn't know whether it was proper, but frankly, I didn't care. I asked Mujah if he'd like to go fishing. He would. He fairly bounced from the room.

I drove to his house later and asked his mother. She seemed surprised, but she gave permission. Then I saw little David peeking from behind her, so I asked for him, too. Mujah was so excited he didn't get much reading done on Thursday, and everyone in school knew about his coming adventure.

"I guess it wasn't fair to ask only him," I told the principal.

"No," she nodded. "But you can't ask all of them. Besides, he's a very special little boy."

Stern and businesslike though she was, I knew that Dr. Mary Phillips Cotter had a soft spot for all of her three hundred students.

Our shift ended on time Saturday, and we split up to go gather our boys. We met at a shopping center on the north side of town. Everyone piled into Don's van or the captain's station wagon. We got to Don's favorite fishing hole a little before noon.

The boys scattered to the four winds. Don tried to show me how to flip the fly rod, but I don't have patience for that sort of thing. Pretty soon I'd abandoned the stream while I helped Bryan and David hunt for animal tracks.

Luis had brought a nephew along. Pretty soon he and the older boys were wading in the chilly, springtime water. Before long, the kids were all soaked. they stripped to their underwear and splashed around while the old timers, on the bank, lay in the sun wondering how the young ones could stand that cold water.

Evening shadows grew. We toweled the younger kids off, dressed them in dry clothes, and waited for the captain and Luis to finish the feast they'd been preparing in a half dozen Dutch ovens. It was dark by the time we finished eating, but a nearly full moon was rising over the ridge east of us.

Captain Meaker pulled his guitar from the station wagon. We sat until nearly midnight singing and telling stories. There was something about that evening. Something about lounging beside the singing stream, watching the trees silhouetted against the sky, David asleep with his head on my lap, and Mujah curled up beside me that brought out a feeling I'd rarely felt before.

Just before he fell asleep Mujah squeezed my hand. He said, "Mr. Boot, this is the very best time I ever had in my whole life!" Then he went to sleep, still holding my big hand in his small one.

Captain Meaker sat watching us. "They sure look small and vulnerable when they're asleep, don't they? Kind of makes me want to run out and gather up all the little waifs I see on the streets and take them home to protect them from all the cruelty and hardship the world has lying in wait for them."

"Yeah," I answered. "But you can do just so much."

He nodded. "Yes. Frustrating, isn't it?" Then he began to pick at his guitar and began to sing very quietly. I'd never heard the song before, but I'll love it all my days. . . "A poor wayfaring man of grief, has often stopped me on my way, and sued so humbly for relief that I could never answer nay. . . ."

I sat and listened. When he finished I said, "That was beautiful."

"It's my favorite. I guess I sort of try to live by it. They say the Savior walks the earth occasionally—disguised. I like to think it's not just a legend."

"That explains a lot."

"About what?"

"About you."

He laughed. "Yeah, maybe it does."

. . . .

We rolled the boys into their sleeping bags; and while the other men crawled into theirs, I lingered by the fire. The night was so calmly beautiful we hadn't bothered with tents. Finally I turned from the fire and walked toward the stream. I'd spotted a small grove of trees along its bank, a little way upstream, and I had decided that was the place.

Moonlight dappled the earth with shadows of new leaves. I scraped away a litter of leaves and twigs so I could kneel. I don't know how long I was there; but by the time I walked back down and crawled into my sleeping bag, I had the answer I'd been looking for.

Chapter Twenty-Two

Let's see, that fishing trip was toward the end of May.

Linda was ecstatic when I told her what I'd done and what I'd decided. We called the Meakers and they called their Bishop. He began making the arrangements. We'd meet with the missionaries a couple more times. Then we'd meet with the Bishop of the ward we were going to join and meet with our Stake president. Baptisms, they told us, were held on the first Saturday of every month, so we set our date for the first of July. My mother took another deep breath when we told her, and we gritted our teeth, waiting for my father to find out.

July seemed a long way off.

Things got busier as summer heated up. We started running on brush fires as spring grasses dried out. Natives of the South Valley became more and more restless as days and nights became hotter. Knifings and shootings began their annual increase. Community firebugs filled their gasoline cans and we spent less and less time in quarters.

It may seem strange to one who has never ridden a big red truck, but the constant string of emergency situations became routine. Very few of them stand out in my memory. But, even so, I discovered that there are pressures—emotional impacts—on emergency service workers that only others like us can understand. Ordinary people can't imagine some of the things we must face from day to day.

One of the things we faced that summer will be lodged in my memory forever.

We'd just finished lunch, on a hot summer day, when our tones hit. "Engine Five. An EMS call. Child hit by a truck. 3800 block of West Ladore. 3800 block of West Ladore. Use channel three."

West Ladore was about a half mile away. Nothing prepared us for what we'd find there. I first suspected something as we slowed and the captain said, "Oh, my God! Oh, my dear God!"

Then I heard his voice over the radio speaker. "Dispatch. Engine Five. Cancel the ambulance. We have an obvious nine-oh-one."

I swung down to look. I saw a mother kneeling in the road, rocking back and forth, screaming, trying to pick something from the roadway. She was literally covered with blood. I stopped, shocked, and I looked more closely. For a moment, I thought my knees were going to go out from under me.

The mother was trying to pick up what was left of a child—a child completely flat on the pavement, lying in a spreading pool of redness. The only way to recognize what had once been a human was by clothes mixed with the gore.

Captain Meaker stood by the cab door, holding on, trying to steady himself. I took a few steps, then turned behind a Highway Patrol cruiser. I leaned against the trunk with both hands while I lost my lunch and what was left of breakfast. A city policeman was there—doing the same thing.

When I could, I took a few deep breaths and started toward the captain and Luis who stood by looking at the mother. "Take her inside a house, Booter," the captain ordered.

Luis and I had to pull her away and fight with her in order to lead her toward a porch. A policewoman joined us. She was crying. I remember only bits and snatches of what happened next. I remember the television camera thrusting its lens toward us. I remember starting to yell. I remember ripping my helmet off and throwing it as hard as I could at the man who was trying to stick a microphone into the mother's face. I'd have hit him in the head with it if he hadn't raised his arm to protect himself. My helmet bounced off and landed on the grass.

I turned the sobbing woman over to a couple of neighbors and walked back out to the street to help with what had to be done. By the time I got back, someone had covered the child with a sheet—but the red was soaking through.

The medical examiner arrived, took a look, talked to a couple of cops and drove off. A police sergeant walked over to us. "Will you guys bag her?" he asked.

"Get the scoop shovel," Captain Meaker said. "That's the only way we'll get her up."

By the time they lifted the sheet I was ready for the job I had to do. I was about halfway through when a police car pulled up. A man wearing a gasoline company's uniform got out. He sagged backward into a policeman's arms when he saw what was on the road.

"Who's he?" I asked the cop next to me.

"The truck driver. They've got him for hit and run."

"Did he even know he'd hit her?"

"I don't know. They're questioning witnesses now."

We finished the job.

None of us ate supper that night. About nine o'clock a white department car pulled onto the apron in front of the empty side of the engine bay. The Department Chief himself got out. He came in and asked for me.

He led me back into the captains' office and closed the door. "Well, Boot," he said, "I hear you bounced your helmet off Kirk Wilson from Channel Three this afternoon. The mayor's upset as all get out."

I nodded glumly. I figured I'd get some days off, at the very best.

The Chief went on, "So I told him I'd talk to you about it. You know you used some mighty poor judgment, don't you?"

I nodded.

"The whole thing is going to be on the ten o'clock news."

I nodded again.

"What was he doing? Trying to interview the mother?" His voice mocked a newscaster's style, "Pardon me Mrs. Jones, can you tell our viewers how you feel about your little girl squashed flat on the pavement?"

I nodded once more.

The chief stood up. He put a hand on my shoulder and squeezed. "So, Booter, I want you to remember just one thing. Next time bust the damn camera first. . . then beat the Hell outta the bastard. Y'got that?"

I grinned and nodded.

"Good," the chief said. Then he added, "Y'know who I feel the sorriest for in all this? That poor truck driver. Witnesses told the cops the little girl ran out from between a couple of parked cars and right under his tractor duals. He didn't know anything about it until the cops stopped him a couple of miles away. You think *you're* going to have trouble sleeping tonight? Just think of that poor guy!"

Then he stomped off down the hall, climbed into his white car, and drove away.

I didn't bother to watch the news that night.

. . . .

But there were some better things that happened that June. I'll always remember the evening when I walked in from watering the garden and found Chief Halvorsen walking in the front door. He was grinning from ear to ear. "Where's Dave?"

I followed him out to the garden where the others were weeding. "Dave!" he called. "Have you heard the news?"

The captain stood up. "What news?"

"I just got a call from Brother Frawley, our Regional Representative," Chief Halvorsen was practically shouting with excitement. "The announcement just came out of Salt Lake. Through President Kimball and the Brethren, God has granted the Priesthood to *all* worthy male members. . . including *you,* my dear brother!"

Captain Meaker just stood there, his mouth hanging open. Then he stammered, "Really?"

"Really!"

"Are you *sure?*" There was pleading in his voice.

"Absolutely! As sure as you and I are here and God's up there."

Captain Meaker stood silent. Then he shook his head and said in a whisper, "Oh, my God. . . my God. Thank you. Thank you!"

Then he burst into tears.

Chief Halvorsen hugged him. He was crying, too.

It must have been quite a sight—five tough firemen standing in a garden—all hugging one another and crying.

I wonder if anyone saw us.

Chapter Twenty-Three

That following Sunday, we went to church with the Meakers. It was one of the happiest days I can remember. Luis and Don were there with their families. So was Chief Halvorsen. Funny, I hadn't known before that night in the garden that he was LDS. I found out, then, that he was president of the Valley West Stake in the western suburbs. All of a sudden, I realized I'd stopped saying "Mormon" and had started saying "LDS."

No one left the chapel after Sacrament meeting ended. A huge crowd of men gathered around a chair in which sat Captain Meaker. They all tried to place their hands on his head, and Chief Halvorsen ordained him to the Priesthood and made him an Elder.

Then, with tears streaming down his face, the captain ordained his son, David, and made him a Deacon.

It took nearly half an hour for me to fight my way up to them, so I could shake their hands. I asked the captain, now that he had the Priesthood, if he'd baptize me the next week.

. . . .

Like I said, things were moving fast that summer.

That next Wednesday I was under Linda's car, working on the brakes, when she called me to the telephone. I answered. A little voice, calm but scared, asked, "Mr. Boot?"

I recognized Mujah's voice. "What's wrong?"

"She did it. She shot herself. I think she's dead."

"Did you call the police?"

"I don't know how," came his reply. "You gave me your number, so I called you."

"Where are you?"

"At the gas station."

"Which one?"

"The one with the red star." I knew the one he meant.

"Where's David?"

"I brought him with me. He's right here."

"Where is she? Where's your mother?"

"At home. In the kitchen." His voice was flat. There was no emotion. He sounded tired.

"Stay there. I'll be right over."

I hung up, called to Linda, rattled off the address and told her to call the fire department and police. Then I jumped into the car and sped off as fast as I dared.

Mujah and David were standing beside the telephone booth when I rolled up. I got them into the car and drove around the corner. Engine 5 was parked in the street. A police car sat beside it and behind that was Paramedic 3. I parked and walked to the front porch. Captain Harris was coming out.

"What are you doing here?" he asked.

"Little kids here are friends of mine. From the school."

"Well, she's not doing too well. Put a twenty-two slug into her belly. I don't think she really wanted to kill herself, but she's on her way out. She's so big the MAST trousers won't fit and we're having trouble moving her. I think she got an artery."

I went back to the car and sat with the boys. They were silent and still. Only David moved. He crawled onto my lap and started to fall asleep. Mujah sat quietly beside me—silent, except when he'd repeat to no one in particular, "What'll happen to David and me?" I didn't say anything, but I was doing some pretty heavy thinking.

She was completely covered when they finally rolled her out.

A police sergeant walked to my car. "You got the kids in here?" I nodded. "Could you take them downtown? Juvenile is on the third floor."

I'd known for half an hour what I was going to say then. "How about if I take them home with me?"

He shook his head. "That has to come through Social Services. First stop has to be Juvenile."

I drove downtown and led them to the third floor where I called Linda, then Captain Meaker.

When I explained to the captain that I needed his help he said, "Well, I do know some people in Social Services who will probably help. But are you sure you really want to do this?"

The question surprised me. "Of course I do."

"I just wanted to make sure you've really thought it through. You know it's not something you can decide, tomorrow, was a mistake. Being a foster parent is even tougher than being a real parent. Have you talked with Linda?"

"Not yet."

"Well, you'd better. While you're at it, maybe you'd better do a little praying, too."

I'd forgotten about Linda. I just assumed she'd go for it. I realized I was making a pretty big assumption. "I'll call Social Services for you," the captain was saying. "Holler if I can do anything more."

I mumbled my thanks and waited for Linda, my mind racing.

It took her nearly half an hour to fight her way through rush hour traffic. But she took one look at frightened Mujah, who cradled David's head on his lap, hugged me and said, "Yes. I know what you want, and the answer is yes."

There wasn't any need to pray about it. Three hours later, David and Mujah were sipping hot chocolate in our kitchen.

. . . .

I drove over to their house and loaded four shopping bags with clothes. When I got home, my mother was sitting in the kitchen with Linda.

"I'm worried," she said when I walked in.

"About what?"

"About what your father will say when he finds out you've taken in two Black children."

Hair on the back of my neck stood straight up. "Mother," I said, as nicely as I could, "I don't really care what my father thinks! We're trying to be good to someone who needs our help, and if he hasn't room in his heart for that. . . then that has to be his problem. . . not mine!"

She nodded silently. "They *are* cute kids."

Captain Meaker helped make arrangements for a funeral for the boys' mother. Reverend Thomas, the Black minister I'd met a few months earlier when the old woman was knocked down in her home, conducted the services in a little store-front church. It was held on Saturday morning, and hardly anyone was there. The boys sat silently through the services. Since then, they have hardly mentioned their mother.

I worry about that, sometimes, and wonder what must be hidden deep inside them.

. . . .

After the funeral, we drove to the stake center at Richland and 34th. Luis met us in the parking lot and led the four of us inside. After we changed into white jumpsuits we were taken to the Relief Society room. There were prayers, music, brief talks—none of which I heard because I was too busy with my own thoughts.

Don led us down the hall to the baptismal font where Captain Meaker waited, also dressed in white. "Is it warm?" I joked, feeling just a little nervous.

The captain dipped a finger in the water. "Just right!"

A moment later Linda waded in and Luis baptized her.

It was my turn. The captain and I entered the water. He stood beside me, gripped my wrists the way Don had shown him and, with his voice shaking as badly as his hands were, he said, "Michael James Joseph Piotrowski, having been commissioned of Jesus Christ, I baptize you in the name of the Father, and of the Son, and of the Holy Ghost. Amen." Then he pushed me under the water.

When he pulled me up, he was grinning from ear to ear, but there were tears in his eyes, too. He pulled me tight against him and whispered, "You can't imagine how good it felt for me to be able to do that. . . or how nice it was that I could do it for *you!*"

"Thanks," was all I could say.

He let go of me and laughed, "Y'know, you're going to make a fine Mormon!" He motioned toward Mujah and David who were watching from the front row. "Look at that. An instant family!" I laughed with him as he added, "And, y'know something else? You're going to make a fine Bishop, someday."

"You can call me when you become a Stake President."

"You're on!"

We changed and returned to the Relief Society room where Don, Luis, the captain, Chief Halvorsen, and the Bishop laid their hands on our heads while Don confirmed us and gave us the Gift of the Holy Ghost. I have to admit that I *was* a little disappointed because I didn't feel fireworks going off inside my chest. There was just a gentle, warm feeling there that let me know I'd done the right thing.

Then we all went out to dinner at the best steak house in the city.

Chapter Twenty-Four

It was the hottest day of the summer. The thermometer on the station's porch was well over a hundred when the tones hit. Don pulled a run card from his pocket and waited for the dispatcher to speak. "I hope it's a false alarm in an ice factory," he said.

"Engine Five, Engine Twenty-two, Ladder Twenty-two, Battalion Three. State Street at Southern. State Street at Southern. A vehicle fire. Use channel three."

State Street and Southern is in Station 4's territory, but they were out on another call. I knew we had a long way to run. We hadn't gone far when I heard the dispatcher again, "Units responding to the alarm at State and Southern, be advised the vehicle involved is a large tank truck carrying Liquid Petroleum Gas. Police advise the vehicle is on fire."

I tensed. Captain Meaker called through the open partition, "Boot, we'll want lots of water. Lay doubles when we get there! Luis, we'll use the monitor."

I reviewed what I knew about fighting LPG fires. Liquid Petroleum Gas is dangerous. It's carried under pressure in steel tanks. Fire against the outside of the tank increases the pressure inside. Usually the extra pressure is blown off through a relief valve, but if flame impinges on the tank for very long it may cause the tank to weaken and rupture. The result is what we call a BLEVE—a Boiling Liquid Expanding Vapor Explosion.

I remembered that a couple of years earlier a railroad tank car BLEVEed in Kingman, Arizona. It killed fifteen men. Thirteen of them were firefighters. Half of their volunteer fire department went up that day.

I also knew that, given a choice, firefighters should let LPG fires burn themselves out. But this one was at the intersection of two of the city's busiest streets—surrounded by highrise office buildings. We had no choice that afternoon.

Don slammed to a stop beside a hydrant opposite from where a ten-thousand gallon tanker lay on its side with flames curling around it. I snagged double lines to the hydrant while Don engaged the pump. Luis was topside swinging the monitor toward the fire.

"Fire's mainly under the cab. Only a little of the tank is impinged!" he shouted as I scrambled up beside him.

I looked around. The tanker had hit a utility pole. Electric wires had snapped and fallen on it. Sparks must have ignited fuel spilled from the tractor. The sidewalks on all sides of the intersection were crowded with spectators. The crowd ignored pleading police officers who were trying to move them back. I knew that a BLEVE from the tank would create a fireball a quarter mile in diameter. I couldn't believe the onlookers didn't see the danger for themselves.

"Stupid idiots!" I yelled.

Luis shook his head. "They just don't know better. Here's excitement, so they're going to watch it."

Water was pouring from the monitor. Luis adjusted the stream pattern to tight fog and aimed it toward the front end of the LPG tank. Just then the relief valve opened with a roar like a freight train. A cloud of white vapor rolled toward us and then ignited into a roll of fire that almost enveloped us. The roll of fire died almost immediately—replaced by a column of fire nearly seventy feet tall.

Luis ducked and held on to the monitor. I don't remember jumping, but I suddenly found myself rolling across the hoses packed in the bed behind the monitor deck. Don and the captain crouched beside the pump panel.

I crawled back up to the monitor. Luis grinned and yelled, "Woweee! That'll sure pucker up your whole body, won't it?"

"Gets rid of the crowd, too!" We both laughed as we watched spectators fleeing in all directions.

Luis moved the spray back and forth over the tank, cooling it until the pressure inside dropped and the relief valve closed with a bang. He directed the stream back to the fire under the cab and snuffed it in a few more seconds.

I was still shaking when I got down off the Engine.

. . . .

Linda invited the captain and his family for a barbeque the day after that LPG call. We were sitting beside the apartment complex pool watching the kids swim while meat sizzled over hot coals. The captain was basting the spare-ribs with another dose of his secret barbeque sauce when I looked up and muttered, "Uh, oh! Here it comes!"

Captain Meaker looked up. "That's your dad, isn't it?"

"Yup."

Dad roared through the gate and stopped next to the charcoal pit. I could tell he was drunk. He started shouting, "So you went and did it, huh? Turned your back on all I gave you. . . all I taught you and joined some. . . some damn *nigger* church!"

I moved toward him. "Dad. . . ."

"Don't you 'Dad' me, you son of a . . . . No, it's not enough for you go an' join their damn church, you gotta rub my face in it, dont'cha. Gotta rub my face in. You invite them jigaboos here for supper, but you don't invite your mom or your dad!"

"Dad. . . ."

I had moved too close. He swung at me, but I saw it coming and ducked. That made him even angrier.

Mujah and David Meaker were standing beside the pool, looking on with wide eyes. Dad spotted them. "These the two little Black bastards you took in your house?"

He moved toward them. The boys tried to back away but the edge of the pool stopped them. "You think I'm gonna let *them* call me 'Grandpa?' You think that an' yer crazy, boy!"

He moved still closer to the boys, snarling at them. "You little Black bastards! You'll never call me 'Grandpa!' You got that. . . .?"

He raised his hand as if he was going to slap one of them. I started toward him, but the captain got there first. He grabbed my father's arm and jerked it around behind him in a half-nelson and lifted him completely off the ground.

"Whoa, there pardner," he said. "Let's leave the kids out of this."

Dad began roaring and struggling. My father was a big man, but he was helpless in the captain's powerful grip.

I stepped over to them and grabbed my father's other arm. "Let's get him out of here," I said. "The kids don't need to see this."

We walked him to the parking lot and shoved him into his pickup truck. I tried to talk to him, but he wasn't listening.

"Dad. . . . please listen, Dad."

His face was florid. "No, *you* listen, you . . . ." He cut loose with an avalanche of epithets. "*You* listen! Don't you *ever* come around my house again! You got that? And stay away from your mother, too! You don't belong to us! You don't belong to us any more!"

He slammed his truck into gear and roared into the street, shouting something I couldn't understand.

I leaned back against a car. I was shaking, but I didn't feel any emotion. I'd been expecting it.

Captain Meaker and I caught our breath. Then he said, "I'm sorry. But I was afraid he was going to get rough with the kids."

"No, you did the right thing."

"But maybe I should have waited a second or two."

"And let him slap one of them into the swimming pool?"

We started walking toward the pool.

"Boot?" The captain was almost whispering.

"Yeah?"

"I lost my family for awhile when I joined the church."

I stopped walking. "You did? Why?"

"My father thought I'd joined Uncle Tom. He put me out on the street."

"I'm sorry. . . . "

"Don't be. It took a couple of years, but he finally forgave me. We were good friends again before he died."

"You don't know *my* father," I said.

"No, I don't. But we can always pray for the best."

We walked back to the pool and tried to salvage what was left of the evening. It didn't work. My father's visit had left a pall over all of us.

The Meakers left early but just before they drove away the captain said, "Oh, by the way. I'm going to take some time off. Ellen and I are taking the kids and going to the Mesa Temple, to be sealed."

Linda said, "That's just great."

Ellen Meaker laughed. "Oh, Linda. You don't know how great it is. It's something we've waited and prayed for for so long. . . and now it's hard to believe it can really happen!"

The captain grinned. "Can you imagine that? She actually thinks she wants to spend all of eternity with *me!*"

She snuggled against him. "I can't imagine a better man. . . ."

They laughed together. Then, as the captain started his engine he motioned to me. "Boot, Mujah was a little shaken by that episode tonight. Maybe you'd better have a talk with him and David tonight. Give them a little reasurrance. Let them know you're still on their side. . . .?"

"I will. And thanks. Thanks for just being here."

He reached out and gripped my hand before he drove away.

. . . .

Mujah, David, and I had a long talk that night before sleep came for them. Linda and I lay awake for awhile; and as I held her, I offered a little thanks that we had only a year to wait before we could be sealed.

The scare I received when that relief valve let go had made me realize again how fragile a hold we all have on life.

Chapter Twenty-Five

Ellen and the captain took a long vacation. A second honeymoon, they called it. Chief Halvorsen laughed, "Only Mormons would take a second honeymoon with six kids."

They got home just in time to put the kids back in school.

In our family, Mujah started fifth grade in a new school, with misgivings, while David entered a private preschool with genuine gusto. Linda had accepted a first grade teaching assignment at a school clear across town. I was only a week away from finishing my probationary year, although I was dreading the possibility of assignment to another station.

Captain Dan Cunningham had filled in for Captain Meaker. Cunningham was a chain smoker and a hard driver. It was a relief to have our captain back.

We'd spent that first day, with our own captain, down at the Academy grounds running Engine 5 through her annual pump tests. We also put ourselves through semi-annual company evaluations, under the watchful eyes of the training staff. We were a little weak on our ladder work, so we left with orders to drill on ladders.

We were about half-way back to Station 5, still in Station 22's territory, when Don shouted, "Whooooeee! Look at that!"

I swung around and looked ahead. A huge mushroom of black smoke was rising not far ahead. "Shall we take it in?" Captain Meaker asked.

Before I could answer, "Let's go!" he was on the radio calling dispatch.

"Dispatch. Engine Five is responding on a loom-up of heavy smoke that looks to be south of Iverson in the vicinity of 23rd West."

"Ten-four," the dispatcher said. "We're getting an automatic alarm on it now. Be advised it's the Van Pelt Paint Company, 2438 South 24th."

We were first in and downright jubilant because we'd skunked Twenty-two in their own back yard. I laid doubles and ran up to the Engine. Smoke was pouring from one end of a long cinder-block building with a balloon roof. Fire was already venting through a roof air conditioner. A two-and-a-half-inch hose was stretched from our Engine through a side door.

I was just pulling on my air pack when a man ran up to us. He shouted, "We've got a man inside! We can't find the forklift driver. He was right where the explosion was!"

I ran along the hose, following it up to the captain and Luis through the heavy smoke. "There's a man missing in here!"

"I know it," the captain yelled back. "But we're going to look for the fire. Twenty-two's going to take the search." There are two methods of rescue: remove the victim from the fire or remove the fire from the victim. The captain had chosen the latter method.

I could feel heat on my face, but I couldn't see fire. That's eerie. The end of the building we crawled through was filled with rolls of roofing paper that burned with heavy, black smoke. I couldn't figure out how it had become so intense so quickly. (Later we learned that the fork lift snagged a temporary electrical wire near a paint mixing vat. Sparks ignited thinner in an open-lid vat. That vat burst into flame and took two other vats with it. The forklift operator had high-tailed it out and watched from a block away escaping without a scratch.)

Luis, the captain, and I were almost completely across the building before we saw a dull glow ahead. We moved forward until we could see a mountain of flame roaring upward into steel trusses and across the ceiling above us. Not far to the left I could see an open overhead door. I realized we'd come in the wrong side of the building.

Luis had the nozzle. He'd just opened up when I saw the roof over us starting to sag. Welded, open steel trusses had lost their strength in the intense heat. I hit the captain on the helmet and pointed up.

He looked and shouted, "Out! Out!" The wall was starting to lean outward, forced from plumb by the collapsing roof's weight.

Luis shut down. We started running for the opening of light at the overhead door. I don't remember hearing any noise. Suddenly Luis and I were in the clear as a burst of flame and sparks rolled through the door. Then the door wasn't there any more—just a jumbled pile of cinder blocks and crumpled roof debris.

I stumbled and picked myself up. "Are you okay?"

Luis nodded. We turned to find the captain. He wasn't there.

The realization hit me like a sledgehammer and must have hit Luis at the same time. We ran toward the flaming ruins trying to protect our faces from the heat with our hands. It drove us back, but we tried again—and again. Fire rolled from under the debris fed by paint pouring from smashed vats.

Finally Luis took command. "Get help!" he screamed.

I ran toward the front of the building while he tried again to beat the inferno. I had almost reached the corner when I met Engine 22 coming around it, laying double hoses. I jumped onto the captain's running board. I began to scream at them. I was half hysterical. All I could do was keep pointing down the building. The captain raised his microphone while the engineer stepped on the throttle. "Battalion Three, Engine captain Twenty-two. We've had a collapse on the south side. We may have some of E Five's men under it. Give me some help!"

It seemed to take forever for them to rig hoses and get water on the pile. As soon as they did, we moved in, digging with our hands, with pry bars, with anything we could get hold of. Heat penetrated my gloves and burned my hands. Then, off to one side, I heard someone shout, "Here he is!"

I moved out of the rubble and back to the side of Engine 22. Somehow, I didn't want to be there when they brought him out. Luis collapsed beside me.

We sat on the tailboard of the Engine while they bagged our captain and loaded him into an ambulance. A television camera was looking at us. I heard someone say, "Firefighters at the scene are in a state of shock this afternoon as they remove the body of one of their own from the flaming ruins of the paint company. Fire

Department spokesmen refused to release the dead fireman's name until his family has been notified."

Luis looked up toward the camera. I noticed wet streaks through the black that covered his face. "We're giving them a good story today," he remarked bitterly.

. . . .

A Division Chief walked up to us. "We'll take you out of service. Why don't you go back to quarters, clean up, and go home?"

Don drove slowly back to Station 5, backed in and shut down the big Diesel. I waited my turn at the telephone and called Linda. She started to cry when I told her. As for me, I didn't seem to have any tears in me. Or much of anything else, for that matter.

We gathered in the apparatus bay and just stood, silent. C-shift started to drift in—recalled to duty by the dispatchers. They didn't have much to say, either. Then the radio speaker clicked on. After a pause we heard the tones of the general call going out. I'd never heard a death call before, but I knew instinctively what was coming. The dispatcher's voice was as calm and emotionless as always. "All stations. The Department regrets to announce the death of Engine Five Captain David Meaker who died in the line of duty at approximately fifteen forty-five hours this date. All stations will lower flags to half mast and will rig out black bunting. All personnel will mask their badges. . . ."

I drove home. We took the boys over to a neighbor's apartment and drove to the Meaker's. We walked in and found Ellen sitting on a couch, surrounded by the children. Linda sat down and embraced her wordlessly. Don and his wife were already there. Luis came in alone a few minutes later. Chief Halvorsen and Chief Eddy had delivered the news to Ellen, and they were still there.

Linda seemed to know what to do and say, but I stood, awkwardly silent, tracing the design of the carpet with my toe. It wasn't until I finally sat down and little Bryan crawled into my lap that I started to cry.

Chapter Twenty-Six

The brotherhood of firefighters is a tight one. Men and women who have faced the dragon and felt its breath are fiercely loyal to one another. And so they came from all over the state for his funeral.

We'd stripped all the hose from Engine 5's bed and made it ready to carry him from the church. When Don stopped outside the Stake Center, the parking lot, lawn, and street were filled. We filed inside and took our places on the stand. Luis and Chief Halvorsen were to speak and Don and I were going to sing.

The chapel was crammed full. The coffin was already in place at the front of the church. Closed, of course, and covered with an American flag. There were no flowers on it—just a medal with a blue and white-starred ribbon. His Congressional Medal of Honor. . . .

The organ started to play. Soon Ellen and the kids came down the aisle. Ellen walked arm in arm with an older woman I could tell was the captain's mother. Kenneth led Bryan who looked around in bewilderment. I couldn't look at them sitting in the front row. I was trying to keep my composure, praying I'd get through the two songs we were to sing.

The opening prayer was offered. The Department Chief spoke. Then Chief Halvorsen. Then Luis. Then Don and I stood and began to sing the slow words of "Going Home." I faltered a few times, but then, I found my voice, took a deep breath, and Don and I finished in full volume. Then we started a song we had sung frequently at the firehouse. An old traditional Black hymn called "Bright Morning Stars Are Shining." I know he liked it because it harkened back to his roots.

We sat down while the Meaker's bishop spoke the final words. That was when Bryan broke away from his family and came up to climb on my lap. He curled up and put his arms around me. "My daddy's in the box," he said. I lost it then. I buried my face against the little boy's shoulder. I wept.

Then, with the men from Station 5's **B**- and **C**-shifts, we escorted the coffin into the bright sun of late summer. As we appeared at the doorway, Departmental bagpipers shrilled a short lament and drums began slowly rolling. A Bat Chief called, "Company! Hand salute!" and many hundreds of firefighters rendered a last honor.

We picked the coffin from its carrier and carried it down the stairs. On the way to the waiting Engine we passed between lines of firefighters who stood rigid at attention on both sides of the long sidewalk. I looked at them as we passed. In the front row were men and women wearing our uniform—their badges all draped. There were men from many companies there—men who'd fought fire with him many times. Dispatchers were there, and clerks who knew him only by his voice on the radio or telephone.

And there were the others. Others who felt the brotherhood and who'd driven hundreds of miles across the state to be there. Some from other cities wore the crisp dress uniforms of paid departments. But most of them proudly wore the simpler uniforms of volunteers with badges draped in black. And some of them, from departments I supposed could hardly afford to buy hose, wore blue denim pants and T-shirts with their department names bravely printed on the back.

They had come because they felt the brotherhood. They, too, had smelled the dragon's breath. They knew. . . .

And, finally, there were the children. I saw them standing near Engine 5 beside Dr. Mary Phillips Cotter. A couple of the boys, imitating the uniformed men and women around them, held their hands stiffly to their foreheads.

. . . .

We lifted him to the empty hose bed and when everyone was ready, in the cars that would follow, Don started the engine and began to roll forward. The massed pipers played a final pibroch. Then a lone piper stepped in front of Engine 5 and led us for a couple of blocks while we walked behind.

Don stopped. Luis and I clambered aboard the tailboard. The other men waited beside the road to ride to the cemetery in cars. The lone piper stepped aside and the lonely wail of his pipe came to my ears as we passed him.

Tears streamed down his face, and I wondered if he had known him as we had.

. . . .

They had dug the grave under a spreading willow tree. The firing squad's rifles cracked. Taps echoed. The medal was retrieved and the flag was folded.

Epilogue

A few months have passed. I still fight fires, but not from Station 5. Don passed his captain's exam and is out in a station on the north side. Luis is studying for his engineer's exam. My father still won't speak to me.

One day last week, Mujah and I were driving when I suddenly realized we were passing a long cinder block building. They were repairing it—putting on another balloon roof with those same widely spaced steel trusses that come down so easily when they're heated up. I made a remark about it.

"Why don't they build safer roofs, then?" Mujah asked innocently.

"They cost too much."

"But what's more important?"

"Dollars are, I guess. After all, does one firefighter more or less make any difference?"

Mujah thought about that for a minute. Then he said, very quietly, "Well, he made a difference to *me*."

I nodded and felt tears sting my eyes. "Yes, he did to me, too," I said. "And to me, too."